Seekers of Earth

The Guardian Knights of Terra, Book One

By Kyle Pratt

CAMDEN CASCADE

PUBLISHING

Seekers of Earth
The Guardian Knights of Terra, Book One

First Edition

ISBN: 978-0-9969412-3-5

Editor: Ben Wolf
Cover by: Inspired Cover Designs

Sign up for my no-spam monthly newsletter
and get a free ebook.
Details are at the end of the novel.

Acknowledgements

Many of my family and friends helped to bring this project to completion.

My wife Lorraine is my first editor, critic, and beta-reader. She reads every chapter several times before anyone else sees it. Lorraine is also my office manager and business partner. Without her support I would not be able to be an author.

I owe a huge debt of gratitude to Doyle McKim, Marcia Jacyna, Robert Hansen, Barbara Blakey, Carolyn Bickel, Debby Lee and Kristie Kandoll for their critique of the manuscript.

Finally, I appreciate my friends Jennifer Vandenberg and Pat Thompson for beta-reading the story.

Thank you!

Chapter 1

On planet Lepeus Delta

Marine Cadet Lucas Baldwin peeked over the top of a boulder, and a blast of hot air slapped his face. Shrapnel fluttered and skipped around him. A sting to the forehead brought a hand to his brow. His fingers traced a thin trail of blood. *Just a scratch.*

The white sun, low in the sky, cast long, dark shadows over the dusty red rocks of the planet making it difficult to see the missile launchers and railguns that fired at them.

On both sides, his men flanked him in the gully. *His men.* He repeated the words as he recalled Lieutenant Wentworth's death mere minutes ago. This was supposed to be a training mission, a first deployment for new recruits and a few officer cadets, like Lucas. The distress call changed that.

Now, at a mere seventeen years of age, it was all real.

Lucas had been running toward Wentworth when the missile hit. Seconds made all the difference. When the dust cleared little remained of the lieutenant. The blast threw Lucas to the ground; the wind knocked out of him, but he suffered only scratches.

He tried to look brave, but it was an act. His heart raced. The men looked to him for guidance. He had none to give.

Another blast shook their position.

Lucas touched the screen of the ethercomm built into the left sleeve of his combat suit. He struggled to sound calm as the captain's image appeared on the screen. "Sir, Lieutenant Wentworth is dead. I'm the only remaining officer, and we're under fire from the Aux base."

The gray-haired captain's image appeared on Lucas's sleeve. "I have told the Auxilium that they are firing upon us, but they have not responded. We are also under attack from the base."

From the ethercomm Lucas heard the alarms sounding on the bridge of the ship in orbit above. Still speaking in the slow, formal tones of his native world, Captain Hawthorne appeared remarkably calm.

Lucas tried to emulate at least the calmness of his commanding officer. "They must think we're Valac."

"I do not see how. We are being scanned by the base on each orbit. They must see that we're a Terran Assault Vessel."

Lucas stared at the communication device. "Why would our allies attack us?"

The captain's image fluttered, and static filled the screen like a heavy snowfall. As the image stabilized, the captain said, "The Valac may have captured the base."

"Yes, of course," Lucas said. "That's a reasonable explanation."

The captain gave a slight nod. "On our next pass over the base, we will fire upon their missile ports. Once they are destroyed, assault the installation. Lieutenant Archer will engage from the opposite side."

Lucas acknowledged the captain's orders and passed the word to his men. He had grown up knowing this day would come, his first day in combat, but he had never imagined it would involve attacking an allied base. He struggled not to shake even as his heart raced. He tried to swallow, but his mouth felt as dry as the dust of this barren world.

A thunderous boom resounded from the base, then a half dozen additional explosions followed. The Argonaut, orbiting above, had launched its attack. Lucas looked over the rocky edge of the gully. He smiled as another blast thundered and the last missile port collapsed and burned.

He clutched his lance and checked the settings. *Charge is green. Set to kill. Fifty rounds loaded.* He looked at his chest and belt. *More ammunition on the bandolier. Knife in the sheath.*

The controls for his uniform shifted to full automatos, providing maximum protection and camouflage. Lucas took a deep breath and locked his helmet in place. As the men on either side of him did the same, they seemed to disappear into the sand and stone behind them. Unfortunately, when they moved they would appear as shimmers.

Captain Hawthorne's image again appeared on a tiny screen on his visor. "Commence your assault, Cadet."

Lucas acknowledged the captain and then turned to the men. "Follow me."

He dashed toward the palace-sized main building. *Did the men follow?* Fighting the urge to look back or check his detectors, Lucas prayed to the God of Earth that the marines chased behind him.

Defensive fire came from a dozen spires along the edge of the base. These automatos towers would fire on any apparent threat.

Concentrating on those dangers, Lucas adjusted the monocular in his helmet for a better view. As Lucas raised his lance and aimed at the nearest spire, the tower burst into flame. Sergeant Collins came alongside firing at the launchers. Others caught up, shooting as they ran.

When they reached the perimeter wall, Lucas fell against it, breathing heavily. What had his father said? *"Less ale and more exercise."*

Father's such a boring old soldier. Lucas struggled to breathe normal breaths. *Still, I shouldn't have partied so much before the mission.*

He thumped the wall with his knuckles. *Carbon crystal*—a common Aux building material, and almost as hard to breach as a magshield. For this small base, 500 Gellers behind the battle lines, it probably seemed more than enough of a defensive wall.

Lucas removed his helmet and breathed deeply. The air of this world held the bare minimum of oxygen that humans needed, but breathing it felt better than the filtered, pressurized air of his helmet.

He tapped the controls on his left sleeve and reported to the captain. "My platoon has reached the perimeter." Looking at the flat plain they had just crossed and the large fortress before him, he felt exposed and vulnerable to enemy fire. "We need to find a way in—or break in."

"Yes." The captain scowled. "And find out what happened to our allies. Why did the base fire upon us?"

Lucas nodded. "Either the Valac are inside directing the weapons against us or they captured the base, reprogramed them, and left."

"I agree with your analysis, Cadet, but either way we need to know."

"Can you send down breaching equipment or climbing suits?"

The captain grunted. "This was only supposed to be a training mission. We have no such gear."

Lucas sighed. "Sergeant Collins, send men in both directions along the wall to find a way in."

The men soon found a large metal door once protected by two defensive spires now reduced to rubble.

Lucas stared at the debris around the door. "Did we destroy the towers?"

"No," Collins replied. "It must have been the Valac."

Lucas examined the door—a typical Aux sliding door. He pointed to a spot in the middle. "Burn through it."

While one of the marines on the breaching team charged the most powerful amplux on-hand, the platoon sergeant had the men gather the remnants of the towers into a defensive arc. Then the marines took their positions behind it, ready as possible.

The breaching team fired the amplux beam at the door. Several minutes later, a spot glowed red-hot under the powerful light.

As Collins finished deploying the men, Lucas walked up to him. "How many men have we lost?"

"Eight, sir, including Lieutenant Wentworth."

Leaving me in charge. The responsibility for both the living and dead pressed upon his mind.

The corporal of the breaching team approached. "Sir, it appears Aux life support isn't functioning. The air inside is the same as outside."

Lucas rubbed his chin. *The Valac can't breathe the air of this planet or the air inside the base of the Auxilium. Perhaps life support got damaged in the battle.* "Keep burning. Get us inside."

The intense light of the amplux soon sent molten metal flowing down the door, but the progress was plodding. The white star now sank below the hills. Darkness grew, and the temperature fell.

Lucas watched the slow growth of the burn hole with concern. The hole had widened a bit larger than a fist. He looked back across the flat expanse they had crossed and at the high wall before them. *We're exposed here. This is taking too long. I should've done something else. What should I have done?*

When he could tolerate his doubts no longer, Lucas used the ethercomm to call his mentor, Lieutenant Archer. In as nonchalant a voice as he could muster, he asked, "Have you been able to enter?"

"Like you, we're using an amplux to burn a hole in a door, but progress is slow. I'll let you know when we enter. You do the same for me."

A cold rain fell from the starless black sky. Finally, the hole widened large enough for a man to slide through. Lucas entered first, singeing his hand on the still hot metal as he did. "Everyone put on your full gear, including gloves, before passing through the door."

He sniffed the pungent scent of ammonia. The Aux atmosphere had once been present. Pressing the sleeve controls, he reported to Archer. "I have entered the building."

"Good job. Are you alone?" Tybalt Archer asked.

"The men are just outside. Why?"

"Get them in, but move forward with care. This isn't a race. My platoon will enter shortly."

Lucas reported to the captain and then did as Archer advised. With lances at the ready, his platoon fanned out along a wide, spiraling crystal passageway. Lucas paused and tried to orientate himself in the complex system of fractal patterns of the Auxilium building.

The few times Lucas had ever walked the halls of such a building, an Aux had guided him. He sighed. "This way, men." *I think.*

The translucent walls of the building, like all such structures, reflected the light and color from every available source. The spiral-shaped edifices sported thin crystals of varying color growing at odd angles. From past experience, he knew these worked with equipment built into the walls, floor and ceiling. The shimmering quality of the surfaces made it difficult to spot passages and adjacent areas.

He rubbed his nose, unsure if the smell of ammonia had grown more intense or if continued exposure was more irritating.

Lucas struggled to navigate the maze of rooms and passages and to stay on some semblance of a course. Even though he knew the overall structure formed a spiral fractal pattern, such knowledge didn't help while attempting to navigate it from the inside.

If Captain Hawthorne is right and this base has been captured by the Valac, we could be ambushed at any moment.

"Stay sharp, men. Watch the flanks." Lucas pointed to chambers on either side. "Check those."

Sergeant Collins came close and whispered. "If any Aux survived, they would have contacted us."

"Perhaps they're wounded or locked themselves in a side chamber. They can survive in this atmosphere for hours and should have breathing apparatuses."

"The side rooms also concern me." The sergeant pointed toward an entrance with his lance. "Some lead to other chambers and connecting spaces beyond that. If the Valac are still here, they could circle in behind us."

"I've been thinking that also." Lucas glanced over his shoulder. "But the atmosphere is wrong for Valac."

"They also use breathing apparatuses."

Lucas nodded. "So what's your suggestion?"

"We should leave and have the ship fire a fission missile into the center of this building."

Lucas nodded again. "I agree, but I don't believe Captain Hawthorne will. He wants to know what happened here. However, I'll forward your proposal."

As he tapped on his sleeve ethercomm, Lucas imagined his father's reaction upon hearing the news. *"I sent you on a simple training mission. All I wanted was for you to get a little experience, but then you go and destroy our allies' base?"*

He pictured his father's disapproving stare. The image burned into his consciousness.

"Why can't you be more like your brother, Victor?"

How many times had he heard that? He shook his head. If Lucas suggested something that killed even one Aux, what might his father do?

To Lucas's relief, the captain said, "No, I don't want to destroy an allied base without good cause. Continue the search with the other platoon. If you encounter the Valac, withdraw, and then we will destroy the facility."

"Yes, sir." Lucas heaved a sigh. "Let's move on!"

For nearly an hour, they spiraled ever deeper into the base without encountering either enemy or ally.

Static appeared on his sleeve comm, followed by the image of Tybalt. "We've found several dead Aux. The wounds look like Valac lance fire."

So there was an attack on the base. "Understood, Lieutenant."

"Is anyone within hearing range of me, Cadet?"

Lucas looked around. "No. Why?"

"Just wondering how the young lord of the realm is doing."

"Stop it, Tybalt. Don't use titles here. I'm Cadet Baldwin now, and I'm…." He frowned. "Eight of my men are dead."

Tybalt's face turned serious. "You made the correct decisions. The enemy killed them—not you."

Lucas nodded. Tybalt had been his lifelong friend, and these last few months, a mentor.

"I'll be there in a few minutes. We are the point of the sword, Cadet."

"Victory our only reward," Lucas said continuing the mantra and hymn.

A minute later one of his men shouted, "A Valac!"

Lucas tensed and then ran in that direction. When Lucas rounded the curve into the next area, the sight of a large, scorpion-like Valac soldier sent his heart pounding in his chest.

Its mandibles arched like giant black hooks in his direction.

Lucas snapped his lance to the ready position.

Even under the goggles of its breathing apparatus, the Valac's elongated bulbous eyes reflected the light of the crystal building and looked right at him.

Four men stood alongside it.

The natural armor plating along its thorax was cracked and broken with the body and stinger tail lying in a heap. It was dead. Still, much of the creature shined like polished obsidian. In training, Lucas had killed and dissected several captured Valac, but he had never before seen one, living or dead, in combat.

Collins walked up to the creature and kicked its fuzzy-haired black head. "See that silver material in the mouth? Aux flesh."

"It was *eating* them?" a wide-eyed recruit asked.

Collins nodded.

Shortly afterward, they found the long, centipede-like bodies of several Aux. Lucas spotted veins of silver, green, and blue under their translucent skin. Stepping around pools and flows of various colored Aux body fluids, He tried to understand what he saw.

The base was attacked by the Valac. The Aux... He shook his head. *...just like the Mage, great with technology, but never good fighters. They must've retreated back into this huge building. But the Valac wouldn't normally land soldiers and fight it out; they would destroy a base like this from orbit. So why was this place so important that the Valac wanted to capture it without destroying it?*

"Let's move on." He shouted to the men. *Maybe the answer is still here—somewhere.*

Several men from first platoon moved along the far wall checking rooms.

Lucas searched the room for Tybalt, spotted him, and jogged to his side. "I wondered when you'd get here."

"We found the base control room. It was programed to fire on anything in sensor range."

"Why would the Aux do that? Had the Valac repro-grammed it?"

Tybalt shrugged. "We shut it down and took the sen-sor crystals." He pointed to his right. "Have your men search that direction. I'll have my men go left, and we'll spiral into the center."

Lucas nodded and headed back to his men.

Concerned that any remaining Valac might be attempting to flank them, Lucas searched several side chambers while Collins took the main body ahead.

Lucas passed through three rooms without incident. In the fourth, an orb at the center of the room slowly rotated and changed colors. The walls reflected the ever-changing light. Several table-like structures held crystal rods, balls, and pyramids.

The floor was a sticky silver mess. The torn bodies of their Aux allies lie scattered throughout the chamber. Several Valac bodies also littered the floor.

His steps made a squish sound as he moved. *Alien legs and blood everywhere.* He stopped trying to avoid it.

Every dead Aux wore breathing apparatus.

The smell... no hint of ammonia in this room. Why would there be a different atmosphere here? What did the Aux have here? Did the Valac take it?

Something moved on his left.

Lucas swept his lance toward it.

A naked human girl, about his age, stumbled in from the far end of the chamber. With her arms and hands she attempted to cover those most private parts. She spoke gibberish, but the tone of her voice and her blue eyes pleaded. Her skin was flawless and as fair as porcelain. Straight blonde hair flowed to her breasts.

How did she get here? No humans serve with the Auxilium, especially not a woman. And why is she naked?

Only then did he realize he was staring, and averted his eyes. His face warmed. He thought to remove his vest for her as he did, one of the Aux near the girl shuddered. Its twin eyestalks rose, and its large eyes scanned the room.

The girl dropped all modesty, picked up a crystalline rod, and, with a great scream, slammed it down on the head of the wounded Aux.

Lucas adjusted his lance, aimed, and shot her.

Chapter 2

On planet Lepeus Delta

The girl gasped and stumbled backward against a control panel. Crystals dislodged, rolled from the pedestal, and shattered, spreading shards across the sticky floor. Stumbling on the wet floor, she fell, hit her head on a pedestal, and landed on the floor with a thud.

Lucas winced, hurried to the girl, and kicked the truncheon aside. Then he moved to the Aux. Life flowed out in a silver stream from its crushed throat. Lucas held the head as the eyestalks went limp and, with a soft whimper, the creature died.

Turning back to the girl, he held his breath. His lance had been set to stun, but his military grade weapon was designed to combat Valac. Seeing the slow rise and fall of her chest, he exhaled.

A palm-sized red circle surrounded the stun probe inches above her bellybutton. He pulled it out and pocketed it. Then he pressed two fingers against her neck and felt the rhythmic surge of the artery. Her heart was good. She would live, for now.

Lucas touched the back of her head. It was sticky and moist. Body fluids of various colors seeped across the floor from the dead Valac and Aux. Was it her blood that matted her hair or the wetness from the floor? Silver, green and blue dripped from his fingers, but no red.

Clearly, she must be insane. Still, he regretted the need to stun her. He covered her with his jacket.

Ackerman and Ely, two marines just older than Lucas, ran in with weapons ready.

"Are you all right, sir?" Ely asked. "We heard lance fire."

Lucas stood and nodded.

"Is that a woman?" Ackerman stepped closer.

"We've only been deployed three months," Ely said. "That *is* what they look like."

Still staring at her delicate face and tangled blonde hair, Lucas sighed. *Why did you kill the Aux?*

The two soldiers flanked him. One asked, "Who is she?"

"I don't know."

He cleared a nearby counter then cradled the unconscious girl in his arms and lifted her from the floor. The jacket covered her front, but he could feel her soft skin against his hands. For now, he wouldn't mention that she'd killed an ally.

"Bring a litter and something to secure her to it. She rambled and swung a rod. She may be insane. We'll lock her in the brig when we return to the ship." *Perhaps death would be a mercy, considering her crime.*

"Aye, sir." The two hurried off.

Lucas laid her on the flat surface of a counter. "What can I do with you until we return to the ship? I could leave you here tied to the litter." He shook his head. With the possibility of Valac still in the building, he shuddered at that option. "I suppose we need to take you with us until we finish the search."

Over an hour later, the marines had worked their way to the center of the building. Lucas stood alone in a mammoth chamber at the center of the spiral structure. Looking skyward, he stared at the multi-color crystal roof at the center. The short night of the planet faded into dawn and illuminated the ceiling.

Just like a stained glass window. A smile grew on his face. He had survived his first combat mission.

Glass crunched behind him. He swung around with his lance ready.

"Sorry. I should have announced myself," Sergeant Collins said. "You did well today, sir."

"Thank you, Sergeant. I guess I'm still on edge."

"That's a good thing, sir."

"Do you have something to report?"

"Yes, sir. The search of the building is complete. No Aux or Valac remain alive." Collins briefed him on the intel they had found. "Everything the men collected is in this bag."

Lucas took the satchel, the same type couriers often used with a long strap and large flap that could be locked to one side. The ship's emblem, a blazing sun with crossed anchors and a trident, adorned the front. As he hung it from his shoulder, Lucas noticed the emblem had torn and frayed at the hem.

"Shall I have the men pull back to the darts?"

"Is Lieutenant Archer ready to return to the ship?"

"Yes, he is." The voice came from behind.

"Tybalt." Lucas turned, and the two clasped arms.

"I'm sorry to hear that Lieutenant Wentworth is dead. Usually it's the new guy that dies." Tybalt smiled.

In his most sarcastic tone, Lucas said, "Since I have *you* as both friend and mentor, I managed to survive."

Tybalt leaned in close. "Your father would be proud."

"I doubt he would say it to me."

The Lieutenant shrugged, and then stood straight. "Did your men collect intel?"

Lucas held up the old courier bag. "All the data crystals we found and vids several of the men made during the search are in here. Also, I have one other item to report." He led his friend from the huge sky lite chamber into a smaller, darker, adjacent room nearby.

As Tybalt walked into the tiny chamber, he turned and cast Lucas an uncertain frown. Then he knelt beside the stretcher with the girl still unconscious.

"Where and how did you find her? Why are her hands tied to the poles?"

Lucas described his encounter with the girl, and that she acted crazy, but left out the part about the murder of the Aux. He wanted to know more about her and why she had attacked one of their allies before risking her execution for murder.

Tybalt grinned. "You always meet such interesting women."

Lucas smiled weakly. *I should tell him the whole truth in private.*

Tybalt pressed the ethercomm on his sleeve, briefed Captain Hawthorne, and requested permission to withdraw from the planet.

"Yes," the captain's voice came over the comm. "As soon as your platoons are onboard, we will leave orbit and head back to base."

Tybalt turned to Lucas. "Let's get off this forsaken world."

Lucas told two privates to carry the stretcher with the girl back to the dart. Before lifting her, he got a blanket from a medicus to better cover her.

Outside the massive Aux building, nine sleek, black Sabre-class transport darts waited with weapons deployed and wings swept out, ready for atmospheric flight. Lucas thought they looked somewhat like menacing birds of prey. Perhaps the designers intended such an appearance.

Around him, dozens of men jogged toward the craft. The seriously wounded went on the first, then the injured, followed by the rest.

Tybalt came up beside him and yelled over the roar of launching craft. "Get on that dart. I'll follow on the last one."

Lucas saluted and ran up the ramp into the cramped shuttle. The girl, still tied to the stretcher, lay on the deck between the two rows of marines. All the men had strapped in except him. He hit the alert button, lifting the ramp and signaling the pilot that all had boarded.

With haste, he secured the hatch.

The craft lifted from the ground as the hatch clanged and clunked into place.

Lucas hurried to his seat as the nose tilted up.

He fumbled with the straps.

The dart shot into the sky and the stretcher, with the girl, slid aft.

Lucas slipped a foot out to hold the stretcher in place. Others did the same. He wondered why none of the marines had tied it down. He hadn't thought of it, but this was his first combat mission.

He looked at the faces of those with him—all young. This was everyone's first combat mission. "We did well today."

Several smiled and nodded.

He hoped it was true for him.

A few minutes later the stretcher floated into the air.

The marines pushed it down and held it to the deck with their feet.

Despite the lack of viewports in that part of the craft, Lucas knew all the ship configurations from school and could imagine the Argonaut as they approached it. The mother ship followed the basic Terran vessel design, a long dark rectangle. Railguns and missile batteries guarded all sides of the outer hull. Two docking bays protruded off the port and starboard sides.

Gravity returned when the dart docked with the Argonaut. A hive of activity greeted Lucas in the cavernous landing bay. Marines swarmed from returning craft and checked weapons in. A medicus rushed the wounded to sickbay and examined minor injuries.

Lucas called over the ethercomm for the doctor. He wanted the girl examined for a concussion, preferably before she awoke and could object. *Maybe she had fallen, and that was why she acted crazy.* No one responded.

Lucas tried again but still got no answer. Frustrated, he looked about for solutions.

Sergeant Collins stood nearby gathering ammunition from the men.

Lucas grabbed his gear and walked over to Collins.

The sergeant took a bandolier from a marine. "Clean that weapon, then turn it in."

"I need to get this to the intel officer." Lucas lifted the bag of crystals. "But I also need a doctor for the—"

"He's dead, sir."

Another marine turned in his lance to Collins.

Lucas stepped closer. "What?"

"One of Lieutenant Archer's men told me. The doctor was headed to the planet to treat the critically wounded when a missile hit his dart."

Lucas imagined his father asking how the mission went. *Well, we attacked an allied base. The doctor died along with eight of my men. Oh, and I shot a crazy girl.*

He gritted his teeth. "I need to get this bag to the commander." He handed his lance and helmet to Collins. "When you're done here, make sure the girl is locked in the brig and then get a medicus to examine her. She may have a concussion from her fall."

"Aye, sir."

Around them, marines stripped off their combat uniforms and tossed them to a helot for cleaning. Two other helots handed out water bottles.

Lucas generally avoided the helots. He'd grown up with servants, but helots, people that amounted to little more than slaves, made him uncomfortable.

But today thirst got the better of him. He grasped a bottle of water from one, and walked on, squirting the water into his mouth and onto his face as hurried down the passageway.

The jump alarm sounded as he stepped onto the oval bridge. Various consoles for communications, damage control, alarms, sensors, helm and engineering ran along the bulkheads. A technician manned each station.

The captain stood at the far end of the compartment talking with the engineering officer. Beside them the holoview displayed the dusty red world below, and then the image collapsed into a swirling mixture of color and diamond-like flares.

Lucas clutched the railing and once again cursed the nausea that swept over him each time the ship jumped. Moments later it faded. He took a deep breath, let it out slowly, and looked for Commander Marin, the intel officer, but didn't see him.

The captain walked past Lucas to the command chair at the center of the bridge.

"Sir, I have intel for the commander, but—"

"Commander Marin is in sickbay." The captain turned his gaze to Lucas. "He fell down a ladder during the missile attack. His leg is badly broken. You and Lieutenant Archer will examine the intel and report to me in the morning."

"Yes, sir."

"That will be all, cadet." He turned his eyes back to the displays.

After being dismissed by the captain, Lucas hurried to his quarters. Entering his tiny berth, it seemed the weight of the Terran Kingdoms slid from his shoulders—at least temporarily.

The courier bag slid from his shoulder onto the bunk. He pulled off the bandolier, removed his combat uniform, and let it drop to the deck. Next, he removed his shirt and pants and stood for a moment in only his underwear.

The air from a nearby duct chilled him. *I'll need to get my jacket back from the girl.* He dressed in a work uniform.

He saw none of Tybalt's gear in the Spartan room they shared. His bunk remained untouched. Lucas grinned. He could relax. Tomorrow would be soon enough to review the intel.

He collapsed on his bunk. For nearly a minute, he lay there with his eyes closed. When he finally opened them, he stared at the light above and thought of as little as possible.

The comm on his sleeve chimed. *I should have turned it off.* Sitting up, he looked at the image. "Sergeant Collins? What do you need?"

"I sent you the Combat Readiness Report for the platoon. When do you want to—?"

"What? Why?"

"Excuse me, sir, but with Lieutenant Wentworth dead, you are the ranking officer."

Why hadn't he realized that sooner? The job didn't end when they got back to the ship. He might only be a cadet, but with Wentworth gone, Tybalt would certainly use him as a platoon officer, at least until they returned to base.

"Of course, Sergeant. Thank you. I'll inspect the men tomorrow after exercises."

He rolled from his bunk, stepped to his small desk, and pressed his thumb to the panel of the computare. The device scanned his face. Lucas adjusted the crystals linking his system to the ship's vid web, and soon a haloview image of the Master-at-arms compartment formed over the desk in front of him.

The privilege of rank—even if I am just a cadet. Going from vid-to-vid, he eventually found the girl's cell.

* * *

Rachel sat against the back wall of what appeared to be a jail cell. Except for a jacket wrapped snug around her, she remained naked. Her last prison, in the crystal building among the monsters, had been warm, but a chill blew through this gray steel chamber.

Neatly folder clothes lay on a nearby bunk, but two soldiers stood just outside her jail cell, watching her through the bars. One man spoke in a calm reassuring voice, but she couldn't understand most of what he said. She pulled her knees close and covered them with the jacket.

This is too real to be a nightmare. Where am I? What is this place?

Tentatively, she felt the back of her sore head and discovered a tender bump. In addition to the bunk, she saw a sink and something that might be a toilet. If it was a toilet, she really needed to use it, but since bars formed one wall of the cell and two men stood just outside, she wasn't going to try.

When she'd awakened, a man in a white smock was looking at her head. He'd probably been trying to help, but she hit him in the face and he quickly left.

Her abdomen itched. Rachel turned to the side, opened the jacket and ripped a bandage from her belly. Beneath it she discovered a red burn mark. She recalled being shot with some sort of stun gun.

She leaned back against the wall of her stark gray cell, and tears welled in her eyes. She rocked back and forth. *Please, oh please, God, don't let me be crazy. How did I get here?*

She'd lain on a table unable to speak or move a muscle. Memories of unimaginable pain mixed with images of unworldly multi-leg monsters.

Rachel slammed her back hard against the cold steel wall. It hurt, and more tears flowed.

One of the men standing outside her cell held out his hand in a stop motion and spoke calmly.

She blinked at him. "What happened to me? Why am I in jail?"

The man looked at her, confused.

Tears rolled down her cheeks. *I've gone mad.* She stared into the distance and rocked faster.

*   *   *

The door squeaked open, and Lucas turned.

Helmet in-hand, Tybalt stepped in to their mutual compartment still wearing his combat uniform. He dropped his helmet on his bunk. "Have you received the C.R.R. from Sergeant Collins?"

"Yes."

"Good." He unsnapped his armor vest. "The captain wants our A.A.R.—"

"Ah… I don't know how to prepare an After Action Report. When does he want it?

"I'll help you. He wants it and a brief on the intel we collected at eight hours tomorrow."

"Eight? We'll have to work all night."

Tybalt shook his head. "No, just most of it."

Lucas turned back to the holo of the still-rocking girl, sighed deeply, and turned off the display. *She's just a lunatic.*

Chapter 3

Aboard the HMS Argonaut

Cool drops ran down Lucas's right cheek. Half awake, he wiped his face. Another drop ran along his brow and down his nose. He blinked. Tybalt hovered over him, with his hand only inches away. A last drop fell from Tybalt's fingers onto his brow.

He sat upright and swatted at his friend. "You let me sleep hunched over my desk?"

"You slept rather soundly—or should I say you slept with great sound. Is there a class young lords take on how to do that, or is it just a natural talent?"

"Huh? What time is it?"

"Seven and fifteen.

Lucas shot to his feet. "We have to brief the captain at eight. I didn't review the intel. What will—?"

"Relax. That's why I let you sleep. Most of the Aux crystals were encrypted, and what I could read was of no value in determining what the Valac might have been looking for. Captain Hawthorne knows you're a cadet. Wash up and get changed. I'll do most of the talking."

Lucas had a sore neck and back, didn't feel particularly well-rested, and his stomach growled. Despite that, he hurried. He ran the autoshave over his thin stubble, combed his short auburn hair, and retrieved his best uniform from the wardrobe. He clipped the gold chevrons, denoting his cadet rank, on his lapel.

Next, he placed the colorful pin emblazoned with the Baldwin family coat of arms on the uniform. The blue shield, with crossed lances, golden lions on the sides, and the crimson motto of his family on top, hung over his heart. Above it sat the golden insignia of the Devonshire Dragoons.

He hurried to the mirror and inspected his uniform. He traced the cut above his brow with his finger. "How do I look?"

"Like a cadet out courting."

Lucas cast him a scowl.

Tybalt smiled and turned to the door. "You look fine. Let's brief the captain."

He hurried into the passageway.

Lucas spotted the intel bag with its red and blue crest in the corner. He grabbed it, caught up with Tybalt, and passed it to him. "You forgot this."

"Oh, thanks. I guess I did."

They made their way up one deck to the senior officer quarters. The marine guard at the captain's door announced them promptly at eight hours.

Lieutenant Archer and Cadet Baldwin entered and stood at attention before the captain, seated at his desk.

The gray-haired captain stared at his palmcomp.

Lucas had never been in the captain's compartment, much more spacious than the tiny compartment he shared with Tybalt. A conference table stood off to the left. Through a door, he glimpsed a couch, a chair, and a table laden with books in the captain's private quarters.

Lucas dropped his gaze to the desk before him. Made from a russet wood carved with nautical designs, it stood wider than his bunk, but not as long.

He missed the luxury of his former, civilian life.

Finally, the captain looked up and motioned for them to sit in the chairs in front of his desk. They sat, and the captain set his device down. "I just finished reading your report. So if we encounter more Valac, the platoon is ready?"

"Yes, sir," Tybalt said. "The equipment is ready. The men are rested. We've lost some good people, but we've gained combat experience." He glanced at Lucas. "Many are young, like my friend here, but they did well."

The captain nodded at Lucas. "Considering that this was supposed to be your first deep space training mission, yes, taking charge after the death of Lieutenant Wentworth, leading the men in combat—all very commendable."

Lucas's face warmed. "Thank you, sir."

"What concerns me is the Valac have not made a major attack in nearly a year." The captain looked at the list of casualties. "Then we receive a distress call and learn they are this far into our territory attacking a minor Aux facility."

"That's certainly isn't their normal method of operation." Tybalt nodded.

"Any ideas on why they would change their tactics?" the captain asked.

Lucas bit his lip, wondering if his opinion would be welcome.

Tybalt shook his head.

"Sir, if I may offer an idea?" Lucas spoke tentatively.

Tybalt cast Lucas a skeptical glance.

"Yes, cadet?"

"It's true that the Valac don't normally take bases. They attack from orbit and try to destroy human and Aux facilities—unless they want something."

"I agree, they wanted something." Frustration lined Tybalt's voice. "But what did they want? The Aux encrypted the data, and we don't have the decryption key."

The captain smiled. "I'm sure command will be able to read the crystals or have the Aux tell them what is going on."

"Well, sir, we do have one more avenue of inquiry," Lucas said. "The girl in the brig is the only living person who witnessed the attack."

"Are you suggesting the Valac wanted her?" Tybalt asked.

"No. Just that she may know what happened."

Tybalt shook his head. "Your own report said she's crazy."

The captain held up his hand and then pointed to Lucas. "Talk to her. See what you can find out. That will be all, gentlemen."

They rose to depart.

"Leave the courier bag, Lieutenant," the captain said. "I'll pass it to the commander when he recovers."

Just for a second, Tybalt hesitated, then he set the bag on the captain's desk. "Yes, sir."

When they entered the passageway, Lucas asked, "Why didn't you want to give the captain the satchel?"

"Don't be ridiculous. I'm glad to be done with it."

Lucas nodded. "Of course." Farther along the passageway he asked, "Do you want to help interview the girl?"

"Oh, I wouldn't dream of barging in on your time with a young lady."

They continued down the passage in silence.

"If she really is crazy, you won't get much," Tybalt said. "But, whatever she says, let me know. We'll prepare the report together."

*   *   *

Dressed in an oversized uniform, Rachel sat on the bunk and sniffed back tears. With one hand she gently rubbed her sore head. *I'm locked in a cell, I don't know why, and my jailors speak some strange language.* She understood some words, but others sounded like French, German or simply weird. She didn't understand enough to communicate.

She struggled to remember how she'd gotten there, but that train of thought led her back to the impossible monsters that had held her prisoner. Tears welled in her eyes again.

Who…what were those creatures? Why did they have me prisoner? She looked around her cell.

Her memories swirled in her head, cloudy, fickle, and incomplete. Considering the horrors she *could* remember, she resisted any urge to explore them further. *God, please help me.*

A soldier came and slid a tray of food through a slot in the bars of her jail cell. He made motions like eating and then walked away.

Since she'd awakened in the jail cell, no one had been unkind, but they didn't let her out either.

Strange smells drifted in the air. Her stomach growled. She walked over to the food.

* * *

The coolness of the compartment surprised Lucas as he entered the brig. He'd never been there before and wondered if they always kept it so chilly. The Argonaut was an old ship and climate control had clearly not been high on the design considerations.

He stopped short of her cell. He could hear movement, but he couldn't see her. If she was insane, he needed to know. If she wasn't a lunatic, her situation remained a riddle.

Why was she on the planet? He recalled their first meeting. *Why had she killed the Aux? Why was she naked?* With that image lingering in his mind, he stepped in front of her cell.

She stood near the bars holding a tray of food, and over an ill-fitting uniform, she still wore his jacket.

They stared at each other for a moment, then she spoke. Her accent and words sounded strange, but he thought she said, "You shot me!"

"Ah... yes." He mimed holding a lance. "I did. Sorry."

She uttered only one word this time. "Why?"

"You had just hit... well, ah." Vids watched this area. He didn't want to say she had killed an Aux. "You were speaking gibberish and acting like a lunatic."

She tilted her head, and her eyebrows furrowed. Again she spoke many words and Lucas understood only one—monsters. Tears seemed ready to flow from her eyes.

For a moment, he wondered whom she called monsters, but of more immediate concern were her tears. He cringed. Then he tried to think of a different approach that might avoid weeping and expand their limited conversation.

Several languages and dialects defined the Terran worlds, and Lucas thought he knew them all, except Asiatic. While it seemed clear that the girl spoke a language and understood some of what he said, they barely managed to communicate.

He decided on a more proper course of action. He'd do what he should've done at the start. He put his hand to his chest. "Lucas." Out of habit, he gave a slight bow as he did.

She pursed her lips, put the tray on the ledge, and then put her hand to her chest. "Rachel." She continued to talk and he listened, understanding little.

However, her words brought to mind a class, mostly slept-through, at the university. He grinned widely. "I think I've figured it out." He turned, took a quick step, and then stopped. "You stay here. Well, of course, you will. I'll be back."

He ran off.

*   *   *

Retrieving her tray of food, Rachel sat on the bunk. *I think… hope… Lucas is trying to help.* She sighed and leaned back against the wall. She scooped up a strange green vegetable on her spoon. *Thank you, God, for this ray of hope.*

*   *   *

In the officer's mess, Lucas set down his tray across from Tybalt and stabbed a bit of brown, unidentifiable meat with his fork. "I'd like you to listen to the girl."

"The lunatic?" Tybalt shoveled in another bite.

Lucas whispered, "That's just it. She may not be crazy."

"I read your report. You shot her because she was speaking gibberish and swinging a pole at you."

"I'd really like you to hear her talk." Lucas scooped up some of the limp vegetables on his tray.

"Why?"

"Because I think she's speaking English."

A mixture of emotions crossed Tybalt's face, ending in a doubtful look. "English is a dead language. Only priests and scholars still use it. How… where would a girl learn it?"

"I don't know, but I think she is."

"Let's assume for a moment she is speaking English. Why would you need me?"

Lucas stared at the ground. "Back at University... uh... the class on dead languages... it was on Monday mornings."

"Yes, as it was for me, also."

"I... uh... Mondays were rough for me."

Tybalt smiled. "Too much merrymaking and womanizing on Saturday and Sunday?"

"Let's just say I didn't learn much on Mondays." Lucas sighed. "I have a vid of Rachel and me talking. Will you listen to it?"

"Who?"

"Rachel. That's her name."

Tybalt pushed back his empty tray. "Lead on, my Lord."

"Stop it."

Back at the room Lucas retrieved the vid. The screen flashed on with the image of Lucas standing at the bars and the girl just inside.

"I didn't pay much attention in class, but I'm sure—"

"Yes. Quiet, Cadet."

Lucas remained silent, but annoyed, as his conversation with Rachel repeated.

Tybalt rubbed his chin and stared at the screen. "How can all of this be happening?"

"Huh? What do you mean, 'all this?' Is it—"

"Her accent is strange, but yes, Lucas, she's speaking English."

Lucas grinned. "Could it be that she's from Earth?"

"That's dangerous talk. I advise caution and discretion."

Tybalt's words hit him in the gut. "All I meant was… well… is it possible?"

"It's far more likely she learned it somewhere." With a sarcastic grin, Tybalt added, "Did you hear? On most planets nowadays they educate women."

"I know that, but—"

"Still, we should keep this confidential until I talk with the captain."

Lucas nodded.

*   *   *

"Reveille! Reveille! Reveille! All hands heave out and trice up. Reveille!"

As the naval hymn played over the vox, Lucas rolled from his bunk and pressed his feet onto the cool deck. As the duty officer read the plan of the day, Lucas washed his face and brushed his teeth, then he dressed quickly.

Tybalt sat on the edge of the bed wearing only underwear and one sock.

"Didn't you sleep well?" Lucas asked.

"I'm fine. You go ahead I'll join you in the wardroom shortly."

With a nod, Lucas shot out the door. It was a great morning. The ship would soon dock in port. He'd done well on his first training mission, and then there was Rachel. A mysterious and beautiful woman certainly made the days intriguing.

Grinning, he continued down the passageway for several yards when the alert signal sounded over the vox.

"Security Alert! Security Alert! Away the master-at-arms force to the captain's quarters! All hands not involved in the operation stand fast!"

Lucas pushed up against the bulkhead as three sailors armed with lances ran by, but he didn't stand fast. He followed.

A crowd had formed at the end of the short passage-way to the captain's cabin. Several sailors, armed with lances, blocked the door.

Lucas pushed forward, through the crowd of officers, to the front. "What happened? What's going on?"

Chief Sadler, the master-at-arms, stepped from the captain's cabin with an ashen face.

A hush fell over the men.

For a moment he just stood there in the doorway, shaking his head.

"Did something happen to the captain?" Lucas asked.

Sadler scanned the crowd. "The captain has been murdered."

Chapter 4

Aboard the HMS Argonaut

U nsure what to do, Lucas watched as Commander Marin hobbled into the wardroom using a cane.

Tybalt stood first and then everyone, including Lucas, quickly came to attention.

"At ease, men," the commander, and now the captain of the Argonaut, said.

Several officers moved to assist him, but he waved them off as he moved along the large central table. "It was a nasty break. My bone stuck right out of my leg. Now it itches all the time and hurts like a lance burn if I put weight on it, but I'll recover. The medicus did a good job."

He limped toward his regular seat, and then stopped and stared at the captain's chair.

Lucas followed his gaze.

By ancient custom and law, when the captain died, or became disabled, the next in line immediately assumed the title and authority of captain. Commander Marin was now captain of the Argonaut, even as he struggled to come to terms with the murder.

"You expect casualties on a combat mission, but this was training. No one imagined we'd be fighting or that good officers and men would die. I never thought I'd take command." He sighed and sat in the command chair. "Captain Hawthorne was a good officer and my friend. Chief Sadler, what have you found out about his murder?"

The master-at-arms set his palmcomp on the table tapped the screen several times, and then read from the screen. "Captain Hawthorne retired to his cabin at nineteen and forty hours. The helot, Adam, was already in the compartment preparing dinner. Adam left at twenty-one and ten."

The vid showed the door open. Adam, a blond-haired man of about twenty, dressed in the simple linen tunic of a helot, stepped out carrying a laundry bag, and a hand lance.

"Then Adam used the lance to stun the marine guard and pulled him into the compartment. Other vids show he went directly to the helot compartment. When the marine guard awoke, hours later, he checked on the captain and reported the murder."

"Where did Adam get a weapon?"

"The lance belonged to the captain and appears to be the one used to kill him."

Marin shook his head. "Adam served the captain for nearly ten years. I've known Adam for five. Why would he hurt the captain?"

"Why did Adam take the laundry with him?" Lucas asked.

A young environmental systems officer chuckled. "Perhaps it needed cleaning."

A few others laughed.

Commander Marin held up his hand. "Silence. I want to hear what the cadet has to say."

Lucas's face warmed. "It doesn't make sense. Kill the Captain and then take his dirty clothes? Also, why stun the marine guard as you leave? The guard was just standing there unaware of what had happened inside. Why bother?"

The commander raised an eyebrow. "Good questions to ask when we interrogate him."

Chief Sadler sighed. "Unfortunately, we can't question him. This happened just before reveille." He displayed a vid of Adam, wearing only his helot smock, opening an escape hatch and being sucked into the vacuum of space.

A murmur of surprise rose around the table.

"A murder and then a suicide?" some asked with a surprised voice.

"Would you rerun the vid?" The environmental officer pointed. "Look. He's still holding the laundry bag. Why would he do that?" The officer looked at Lucas.

Lucas shrugged.

Commander Marin's expression changed from frustration to anger. "We make our final jump to Brittany base in just over three hours." He locked eyes with Chief Sadler. "Have your preliminary report ready for transmission before that last jump. I don't care who you have to interview or interrogate—find out if anyone else was involved before we dock at Brittany."

"Yes, sir."

Lucas leaned back in his chair. "The only one who couldn't have been involved is the girl in the brig."

"Why is she in the brig?" The commander's voice still tinged with anger.

"Uh… we were afraid she was a lunatic," Lucas said.

"Is she?"

"No, sir."

"Then release her."

"Yes, sir."

Tybalt spoke up. "Excuse me, sir? Did the captain give any orders about what to do with the lady when we reach Brittany base?"

"No, why would he?"

"Just wondering, sir."

"When we dock, she gets off the ship and contacts her family." The commander pointed to Lucas. "However, until then, Cadet, you found her, so she's your responsibility."

"Yes, sir. Thank you, sir." *I think.*

"Enough about the girl." Marin's eyes narrowed as he looked around the table. "Every helot and member of this crew will cooperate with the Master-at-arms. If there are conspirators, I want them found before we dock."

As the officers filed from the wardroom, Lucas cast Tybalt a concerned glance. He appeared lethargic and pale. "Are you ill?"

As they stepped into the passageway, Tybalt shook his head. "I haven't been sleeping well since the skirmish. Stress, I suppose."

"If I've been the source of your anxiety, then I reproach myself. I know I'm not a natural warrior like my brother, Victor, but I've tried to—"

Tybalt rested his hand on Lucas's shoulder. "You haven't been a burden. I'm glad your father asked me to mentor you."

Lucas sighed. His father expected him to be the perfect young lord and warrior, but more than anything he wanted to live up to Tybalt's expectations.

"Speaking of family, would you ask your sister to meet us at Brittany?"

Lucas gave him a questioning glance. "Are you courting Katherine?"

"Me? No." Tybalt frowned. "Your father may have secured a title for me, but marry his only daughter? I think he has grander plans for her. Katherine is a friend, and I thought we'd both like to see her after three months in space."

Lucas nodded. "It would be nice to see her, and since the Argonaut will be in repair dock for a few months, perhaps Katherine could come on Father's yacht—without Father."

Tybalt nodded "That's the luxury-loving Lucas I've come to know."

"It will be grand to get away from this ship. I'll send her a message."

As they approached an intersection of two passageways Lucas turned to Tybalt. "Do you have any duties you need me to perform this morning?"

"Normally I'd have you manage the cleaning and stowing of the gear but…" A smirk grew on Tybalt's face. "…why don't you go free your new girlfriend?"

"Don't start any rumors." Lucas felt his face flush. "I still need to interview her about what happened on the planet. Could you come and help translate for us?"

Tybalt took a deep breath. "Only you and I know about the order to question her."

"It's still an order," Lucas asserted. "Why wouldn't we interview her?"

Tybalt stood silent for several moments. "The poor girl is fragile already. Why get her involved in matters of war?"

"As I said, the captain ordered that she be interviewed."

"Yes." Tybalt leaned against the bulkhead. "However, he didn't say when to report back what we find."

"What are you thinking?"

"The ship is scheduled to be in repair dock for three standard months. Let's take that time to carefully interview her. We can give our report when we return."

"But… she may contact her family and go home when we get to Brittany."

"Do you really think she has a home, or family, anywhere in Terra?"

Lucas shook his head.

Tybalt rubbed his chin. "If she does contact her family, we'll hurry the interview. If not, perhaps she could return to Devon with us—and a few guards perhaps—in case she is crazy."

Lucas nodded. "I don't believe she is."

"If that proves true then your sister could escort her on the journey."

"That seems like a good idea. If she does say something significant, we can forward it to command early."

"Agreed. So keep me informed, and go practice your dead language skills."

*   *   *

Lucas trotted down the passageway to the quartermaster's office and knocked on the door. "I need a berthing."

"You have one."

"No, I need a separate one."

The quartermaster cast him a confused glance.

Lucas sighed. "The young lady in the brig. Commander Marin has ordered her released into my custody."

"Only the captain can order someone released from… oh, I guess he's the captain now."

Fiddling with his palmcomp, the quartermaster muttered, "A woman on a warship. By all the kingdoms of Terra, what are we coming to?" He looked back to Lucas. "We have a few open berths now—since the battle. I suppose the captain wants her near you?"

Lucas didn't object to that line of thinking.

Minutes later, Lucas stood at the cell door with the guard. "The captain has ordered your release."

Rachel, still wearing his jacket and a baggy uniform, scrunched her face.

Lucas smiled at her funny look as the guard opened the cell door.

She stood at her bunk with a less comical, more confused, look.

"You're free." He motioned for her to come to him.

"Free?" A smile grew.

"Yes."

Slowly she stepped from the cell. Her pleading eyes fixed on Lucas. She said many words, some gibberish, others familiar but shrouded in a strange accent. Still, he thought he understood "please" and "home."

He shook his head. "We're going to Brittany, but I don't think that's your home. I've been there several times, and they speak Lingua Terra." He motioned for her to follow him. "Where we're going is nicer than the brig."

When Lucas arrived at the compartment, across the passageway from his own, he opened the door for Rachel and stood to the side. It matched Lucas's room, small, gray, and sparse. Two bunks, two small desks, and two chairs took up most of the space. Neatly folded, coarse blankets and sheets sat on both beds.

She made motions as if washing herself. "Bath?"

Lucas moved to a sink attached at the center of the far wall. "This will have to do for now. I'll try to figure out something so you can shower." Lucas imagined he'd have to guard the entrance to the head while she showered. He pointed across the passageway and touched his chest. "My berthing."

After a moment she seemed to understand, then she smiled and nodded.

Motioning that she should stay and that he would return, he bowed slightly, opened the door, and departed.

* * *

Rachel stood in the center of the room trying to make sense of her situation. She'd awakened a few days earlier and discovered herself the captive of unworldly centipede-like monsters. They had laid her on a crystal slab, somehow rendered her unable to move, and examined, poked, and cut her. Unable to even scream, she could only endure. During that time she'd nearly lost all hope and sanity.

Later, she witnessed a battle between monsters. Giant scorpion-like creatures launched stingers at her centipede tormentors who withered in pain. The centipedes fired lasers that burned holes in the giant scorpions.

Terrified, she hid while the battle raged around her. The surviving scorpions tore at the dead centipedes' flesh with huge pinchers. As the battle ended, she believed the last of her sanity had expired, then she saw a ray of hope—a human. But he shot her, and when she awoke in jail, she lost hope again.

She opened the door to her new room and shut it. This room looked a lot like her cell, but at least the door was unlocked. She didn't understand why Lucas had shot and jailed her or why he'd given her more freedom. So much confused and frightened her, but he seemed to want to help, and for that she was grateful.

Rachel walked over to the sink and stared into the small mirror. A sad, disheveled, girl stared back. She looked for a comb or a toothbrush but found none. She ran her fingers through her hair and pulled it back.

On the shelf below the mirror sat a single white washcloth which she used to wash her face. She looked around the tiny, windowless room. Thankful for privacy, she removed the uniform jacket and shirt and washed under her arms as tears welled in her eyes.

*   *   *

Lucas stood in the passageway for a moment. He knew she wasn't a lunatic, but he'd seen her murder an Aux. When he saw the door open, he grew concerned that she'd leave, become hysterical, and hurt someone or herself. Then the door shut, and he relaxed.

After being in jail, it seemed reasonable for her to check the door. A minute later, after he was convinced she would remain, he returned to his cabin. Sitting before his computare, he created a message.

"Katherine, our ship will dock soon. I can't say when or where, but I'm sure you can find out. Could you convince Father to allow you to meet us with the family yacht?" Then, feeling very mischievous, he added, "Tybalt thought it would be enjoyable to sail home together."

As soon as the message queued, he jogged down one level and aft to the marine compartments. First, he checked the operations center. The lights flickered on as he crossed the threshold, a good indication of an empty room.

All the displays were dark. He looked across the room to Tybalt's tiny office. Through a window that allowed his mentor to watch the operations center, Lucas saw that the office was dark. Lucas turned and left.

Next he came to the large, common berthing area where dozens of enlisted men kept busy cleaning everything in the space. Tybalt wasn't there, so Lucas moved on to the storage area where still more marines busied themselves stowing arquebus rockets, launchers, power packs, and ammunition. He still didn't see Tybalt, but he did spot Sergeant Collins at the far end of the compartment. He'd know where to find Tybalt.

Weaving through the multitude of marines toward Sergeant Collins, Lucas spotted Tybalt kneeling beside an ammo box.

"Good, you're here." Tybalt grinned. "Did you get the fair maiden into a room?"

Lucas scowled at his friend. "Rachel is across from our berthing."

Tybalt smiled approvingly. "That's probably a good idea. Did you get additional information from her?"

Lucas shook his head. "No. I understand less than half of what she says."

"You have achieved more understanding of women than most men."

"I'm going to need to learn English—"

"It is best that we not talk about such things here." Tybalt stood. "Take over the ammunition inventory, and tonight we'll discuss plans—alone."

"I'll get a palmcomp from the office."

"No, here, use this one. The inventory is already loaded."

Lucas nodded, took the device, and, when he wasn't thinking of home or Rachel, he counted arquebus ammo.

Women and home had occupied the thoughts of sailors and marines since the time of sailing ships on the Earth of long ago. At night, he didn't dream of distant planets and victory on the battlefield, as he imagined of his older brother, Victor. Right now he'd settle for a soft bed and good food.

Why he thought so much about Rachel puzzled him. Sure, she was pretty, but he was the son of a marcher lord, the Marquis of Devon. Finding attractive female companionship had never been a problem. So why did she occupy his mind? Beauty and the mystery of where she came from, perhaps that was enough to captivate his thoughts—at least until he returned home.

As he shut the ammo box, Lucas looked around. No more containers needed inventoried, and nearly all the men had left the compartment. His stomach grumbled. Checking the palmcomp, he discovered three hours had passed. It was dinnertime.

I should get food for Rachel... or should I bring her to the wardroom to eat?

Lucas hurried to Tybalt's office to leave the palmcomp. The light flickered, but didn't come on as he entered. His hunger propelled him across the tiny familiar room. As he set the device on Tybalt's desk, something caught his eye. Lucas turned on a desk light.

A strap and the corner of a courier bag stuck out from behind a locker. Courier bags weren't common on a ship, and he'd never seen one in this office. When he pulled it from behind the locker, its weight sug-gested it was empty, but he looked inside anyway for confirmation.

Then he noticed the frayed emblem. A cold shudder ran through him.

This is the bag Tybalt gave the captain. How did it get here?

Chapter 5

Aboard the HMS Argonaut

Lucas clutched the satchel as he trudged slowly back toward his berth. The bag had been in Tybalt's office. *How did it get there?* He recalled how tired Tybalt had been in the morning—like he hadn't slept. *The vid showed that no one had entered the captain's quarters or left. He couldn't have had anything to do with the murder.*

Such thoughts amounted to silliness anyway. Tybalt had always been loyal, both to the Baldwin family and to Terra. There must be another explanation.

When he arrived, he stood in the passageway, afraid to find Tybalt inside. *How can I ask him if he's been involved in a murder? He's my friend, more of an older brother than my real brother.*

Any meeting the captain held would've been recorded in the captain's log. Lucas could ask the Master-at-arms about it, but not without raising suspicion.

Should he step into the berth and confront Tybalt, go to the Master-at-arms office and check the log, or stand in the passageway and look stupid?

He decided on a fourth option and knocked on Rachel's door.

The door flew open, and with a combination of gestures, smiles, and unintelligible words, Rachel beckoned him inside.

Lucas hesitated. The gossips tried to make him out to be like his older brother, but he was no rake. While he'd ventured into the bedrooms of a few young ladies, they had pursued him more than he did them. Rachel's reputation concerned him now, but she seemed unworried. So with the knowledge that she was an attractive mystery, not a strumpet, he forced a smile and entered.

Lucas sat in a chair, and to his chagrin Rachel sat on the bed, seemingly unaware of the implied amour.

She continued to speak. By the inflection of her voice, he knew she asked many things, but he understood few of the words and could only guess at the questions.

"Ship?"

Her accent sounded peculiar. "Yes, this is a ship," he replied.

She made wave-like motions.

"No, not that kind of ship." *How do you do a spaceship with your hands?*

Lucas thought of taking her to the observation port, but she would only see the swirling colors of the Mage Tunnel. Instead, he moved the chair to the desk and pressed his thumb to the panel. The computare scanned his face.

He adjusted several crystals, and as he did, a list of messages appeared in the air before him. Most were old, saved for some half-remembered reason, but he noticed a new one from his sister. He tapped the airborne entry and a face appeared.

"Hello, brother."

Lucas turned to Rachel. "This is my sister, Katherine."

Rachel gasped and then smiled. "Sister?"

He nodded and returned his attention to the image.

"Daddy got me my own ship. It's just a big dart, but it's mine. I'll be there when you reach port. It'll be fun, and I can show you my new ship. I'll see you then." The image dissolved.

For a moment, images of home and family flitted through his mind. Then Lucas recalled Rachel's presence. He made the final adjustments to the computare. A halo image of the Brittany solar system appeared where moments before his sister had been.

Rachel stepped closer and gazed at the three-dimensional vid.

"That's Brittany, where we're going." Lucas pointed to a small blue-green ball.

Rachel's eyes widened and she stumbled back to the bed. "Space?"

He understood that word. "Yes, space. The heavens."

Lucas smiled. They were communicating, at least to a small degree. He glanced at Rachel and realized that her wide eyes and gaping mouth expressed not amazement but fear. His smile faded.

For several moments, they sat in silence. Lucas wanted to say something, but he didn't know what. His jacket hung over a chair. He pointed to the family crest and name on the upper left of the garment. "Baldwin, that's my family. My full name is Lucas Nathaniel Alexander Baldwin."

She seemed to understand that the jacket belonged to him and motioned for him to take it.

Lucas shook his head. "If you need it, you can keep it."

She held her hand to a nearby air vent and said several words, but all he understood was, "Warm."

Grasping the satchel from the floor, Lucas stood. Now was a good time to depart. He stood, bowed slightly, said goodbye and, taking the jacket, stepped into the passageway. As she shut the door he flopped the jacket over one arm.

Tybalt, at the far end, strolled toward him. "I hope you finished the ammunition inventory before you decided to take advantage of the young lady."

Lucas felt his face flush, then his anger flared, more so for the insult to Rachel than to his honor. "She is a lady, and I am no libertine. Please try to remember that." A strong rebuke from a cadet to his senior, but he was also the son of a marcher lord.

Tybalt seemed to understand that the noble son, not the cadet, had spoken. "Forgive me. My sarcasm sometimes gets the best of me."

Lucas followed as Tybalt stepped into their berth.

"Come on. Let's get some chow." Tybalt set a palm-comp on the desk, turned, and headed for the door.

Anger still churned within Lucas. He stepped in Tybalt's way and held up the satchel. "I found this in your office. What can you tell me about it?"

Tybalt's eyes widened, but he quickly assumed an indifferent gaze. "It's a courier pouch. What of it?"

"This is the satchel we gave to the captain." Lucas shook the bag. "The crystals we collected at the Aux base were in it."

"There are a dozen such pouches on the ship." Tybalt shook his head. "Why would I have that particular one?"

Lucas ran his finger along the worn hem. "This is not any satchel. This is *the* one we gave to the captain just hours before his murder. It contained intel, but now it's empty. I found it in your office."

"I don't have to explain—"

"You'll have to explain your actions to *someone*," Lucas snarled.

Tybalt laid his hand on his cluttered desk. Slowly he shook his head. "Perhaps some explanation is required." He sighed. "I have long doubted the history we've been taught. What if the wrong side won the War of the Kingdoms? Those poor souls we now call helots might've been right."

Tybalt had lied to him and now spoke sedition. Lucas stepped back, clutching the hilt of his knife. In a voice, louder than he wished, Lucas declared, "That is treason." He drew his knife.

With one arm Tybalt blocked Lucas' knife hand and with his other arm grasped his own knife from his belt and brought it to the throat of Lucas. In a conversational tone, he said, "Calm yourself and listen."

Gradually, each man lowered his knife to its sheath, but their eyes remained fixed on the other.

"I have been your friend and mentor," Tybalt said. "That hasn't changed. I am *not* your enemy."

Lucas kept his fingers on the pommel of his weapon. "Your words are treasonous. Your actions suspect."

Tybalt shook his head. "Truth is an absolute defense. If the girl is from Earth, then we've been told a lie."

"But you haven't sought answers from Rachel. You've avoided her."

"I've shunned her. She alone cannot prove the existence of Earth. While you gained her confidence, I sought answers from the crystals." Tybalt lifted the bag. "I lied when I said most of the data crystals were encrypted. Most are not."

"You still have the intel?"

"Yes."

"Then show me this truth you've discovered."

"The crystals aren't here. Are you willing to follow me to another part of the ship?"

How could his friend and mentor be disloyal? If some truth awaited revelation, he had to see it.

Lucas nodded. Still, he stayed cautious. "Leave your knife here. I'll be the only one armed."

Tybalt stared at Lucas for a moment and then laid his knife on the desk. "Follow me."

As they marched along the gray, utilitarian passageways, memories flowed. Lucas had known Tybalt all seventeen years of his life. Tybalt's father still managed the farms that surrounded one of the largest Baldwin estates. Even though Tybalt was four years older, Lucas had followed him many places as they had played in the fields and hunted and fished in the forests.

He remembered once finding an ancient tree that had fallen across a gorge. Water roared over rocks fifty feet below. Eager to cross, Lucas stepped onto the tree. Tybalt stopped him, insisting that he cross first. Holding limbs and testing each step, Tybalt crept along. Then he returned and led Lucas across.

On the day Lucas's older brother Victor went off to war, military marches had resounded. That morning Lucas had sought Tybalt but couldn't find him. When Victor marched down the stairs, it was the first time Lucas saw him in the full dress uniform of a Terran Knight. Every adult male of any rank wore their best uniforms.

As a child, Tybalt shouldn't have been in uniform, but that day, for the first time, he wore one—the uniform of a squire. Was it Father or Victor who had selected him? Lucas had never found out, but nonetheless, at barely sixteen, Tybalt would go to war.

Before Victor and Tybalt had departed, strong drinks flowed, speeches slurred, and tears rolled down the face of his mother and sister. Lucas had run from the house to the nearby stone chapel. From his earliest memory, the family had gathered there for sermons, holidays, and on the eve of battle. Always his family sat in the front pew, dreadfully serious.

Standing near the altar, Lucas had gazed up at the stained glass window before him. There, a multitude of colors shined through etchings of the Earth and a cross. With tears blurring his vision, he cried. Not for the brother going off to war, but for Tybalt. He feared for him and feared he might never see him again.

For the first time in his life, Lucas had prayed. He implored God to spare Tybalt and return him home to Devon. Tybalt still lived, but he'd never been able to return home. Eventually, Lucas concluded that the God of Earth was as dead as His planet.

Lucas's childhood had ended that day. As reports of battles came back to the family, he worked to live up to the growing reputation of his older brother and Tybalt, the friend who served at his side.

Tybalt descended a ladder, returning Lucas's thoughts to their present dilemma.

When they again stood on the same deck, Tybalt turned. "It's just up here."

Lucas starred at the back of Tybalt's head as he followed. How could his friend and mentor be disloyal?

Still a step behind, Lucas inched his knife from the sheath.

Chapter 6

Aboard the HMS Argonaut

Lucas kept a firm grip on his knife, concealing it in its sheath from all who passed as they journeyed along the gray passageway. Together with Tybalt he had descended three levels to a darker, more humid part of the ship.

Finally, Tybalt pointed down a hatch. "It's this way."

Lucas cast his gaze down a ladder that disappeared into darkness. "That leads to a helot compartment. Why would you hide intel there?"

"The helot computares aren't connected to the ship's web. That allowed me to examine the crystals here without fear of detection."

Lucas stared into the black trying to decide what to do.

"I would never cause you harm," Tybalt said.

"Minutes ago you held a dagger to my throat."

"You drew your weapon first but, if it will help, I apologize. I was afraid."

"You, fearful? Of me?" Lucas stared at him. "I can't imagine it."

"My fear was… is more philosophical."

Lucas squinted at him.

"Do you believe the girl, Rachel, comes from Earth?"

"I don't know," Lucas whispered, staring into the darkness. "She may be."

Tybalt looked both ways along the empty passageway. "If she is, she personifies a truth that some among us declared more than a hundred years ago—the Valac didn't destroy the Earth, and the Mage have lied to us."

"Does it frighten you that it might be true?"

"Truth does not scare me." Tybalt shook his head.

"If not my blade or the truth, then what caused you fear?"

Tybalt's gaze darted up and down the passageway. "What if our ancestors from Earth weren't slaughtered—."

"Why would you fear that?" Lucas slid the knife into its sheath..

"—but before I'm able to prove it, I'm discovered and turned over to Star Chamber? My father... mother, my family will see me as a traitor. And so, in the pursuit of truth, I lose my family and Star Chamber sentences me to life as a helot."

The word "helot" thundered in Lucas' ears. "You've thought this through."

"It deserves serious thought."

Lucas nodded. He'd lived a life of luxury, power, and wealth, but the course he had embarked on could rip that all away. Fear and history jumbled in his mind.

Over a hundred years ago, the Duke of Grafton had proclaimed that the Mage had lied, that the Earth hadn't been destroyed, that it was still out there, somewhere, beyond the known worlds.

The War of the Kingdoms that followed the duke's proclamation was short, but brutal, and ended with the burning of Grafton at the stake. Beyond that, seven generations of his many followers were condemned to life as helots.

Today, cadets trained using Grafton's likeness as a target. No one would believe the duke spoke the truth.

Lucas shook his head and edged away from the ladder. To live as less than a serf, stripped of honor, enduring endless toil, and to die without a family name or world he could call home... that was a price too great to bear. He stared at the hatch and the darkness beyond, unable to approach.

Tybalt stepped to the ladder. "All I can promise is that I *will* find the truth. At first I wanted to keep this from you, but since you've learned so much on your own, I'd like you to be a part of the discovery. If you cannot, I beg you, do not betray me or the others."

He disappeared down the hatch.

"Others?" Lucas stood, unable to move.

He could imagine the tears of his mother, the disappointment in the eyes of his brother and sister. He imagined the shouts and curses of his father. *"It was only a training mission, but you decided to follow a traitor and a lunatic girl and commit treason."*

Lucas's hand slid from the knife, still in its sheath. Consumed by thought, he began a slow walk away from Tybalt along a passageway to nowhere in particular.

He didn't know how long he had been walking, but he smelled a meaty broth, and his stomach grumbled. Food always comforted him. Changing direction, he headed to the wardroom.

In the compartment, marine and naval officers mingled in small groups. Stepping to the counter, Lucas caught his first glance of dinner. After three months in space, supplies had dwindled. Apparently the meal was a collection of available foods, accented with salt and spice into a new, undefined stew. Warm and filling, but nothing like the culinary creations of home.

As he waited behind others in line, he watched the two helots who served the food. People. They looked just like him, except he wore a uniform and the Baldwin family crest over his heart. They wore drab gray linen cloaks and had no family name.

If caught, Tybalt might soon face such a fate or be executed.

Lucas gathered two trays and two bowls for stew with ample bread and cutlery.

A helot silently filled the bowls.

He made the short walk from the wardroom to Rachel's door. For the third time that day he stood there, this time balancing trays and bowls, as he knocked.

She opened the door and smiled at him and the food. Then she eagerly waved him in.

As he stepped inside, she pointed to a holoview display. Rachel had recalled the data on the Brittany star system. However, the aspect ratio of the holoview was incorrect. The planets had distorted into oblong shapes.

Every child learned how to correct that as they played games on a computare and holoview.

However, if she'd never seen these devices, how would she know? She may never have used them, but she had watched his hands as he did.

He set the food on the other desk and bent over her shoulder to correct the image. "Why are you viewing this star system?"

For a moment she looked confused, then she placed her hand over her brow and gazed at the projection like a lookout staring into the distance. She said four words, but he understood only one: "Home."

"If home is Earth…"

"Yes, Earth! Home!"

He gasped at her announcement. Those weren't the words he wanted to hear from her. His heart pounded. She'd said it—the declaration that could get them all killed. He wanted to flee from the room, and deny he ever knew her, but he didn't. He stared at her and wondered how she could be from that ancestral home of long ago.

Somehow he would need to find out. He would need to find the truth. He shook his head.

"Earth won't be in our navigation charts. Whatever remains of Earth is now deep in the Valac Hegemony." For the first time in his life, he wondered if that was true, but finding truth would have to wait. He moved a tray toward her. "Shall we eat?"

He divided everything into two portions and passed her a tray, bowl of stew, bread, and cutlery.

He ate slowly, casually, while she devoured her food. Lucas wondered if it was hunger or the uncertainty of the next meal that drove her to eat so fast. He passed her some of his bread, which she quickly ate.

After eating, he spent several minutes showing her how to adjust the three rows of crystals that controlled the computare to retrieve information and correct the holographic display.

As he picked up the two trays and bowls to leave, Rachel viewed one system after another, examining the various planets of each.

In the passageway, he paused. Since he first tried to communicate with her, everything suggested thoughtful intelligence, not lunacy. However, she spoke a dead language and considered Earth, a dead planet, her home.

Lucas took a deep breath, let it out gradually, and began a slow walk back to the wardroom. All his life he'd trained for combat. Death on the field of battle remained a real possibility. That never… well, rarely… frightened him, but searching out the truth about Rachel and Earth and the possible consequences? That terrified him.

He returned the trays and other items to the wardroom then walked to the bridge and approached the petty officer at the navigation station. "When will the ship make the final jump to Brittany?"

The petty officer grinned. "I've been asked that many times this watch, sir. In about four hours we'll drop to normal space on the edge of the system. Then we'll get final coordinates and make the short jump to space dock. The jump into the system will only last a few minutes."

Lucas, familiar with the procedure, nodded.

The petty officer smiled. "We could be on shore leave in five or six hours."

Lucas thanked him and left the bridge. Heading aft, for no particular reason, he passed the wardroom and officer berthing, descended to the medical bay, passed the environmental systems, continued down to the cargo and ammunition bays and along several missile turrets. When he reached the aft docking back he reversed course.

Over an hour later he found himself back in the passageway near his berthing, trying to decide if he should go to his quarters, find Tybalt, or knock on Rachel's door. His inability to decide a course of action frustrated him.

Lucas slammed his fist against a nearby control panel, cracking the screen. A trickle of blood dripped from a cut on his hand. Rachel's door cracked open as he licked the wound.

He blinked at her. "Sorry if I frightened you."

Rachel waved him in.

This time he crossed the threshold without hesitation and observed her continued examination of star systems. He moved his chair close to the computare and changed the holoview to display the forward vid image. The swirl of colors and diamond-like sparkle of electrical bursts from the Mage Tunnel the ship traversed snapped into view before them.

Rachel gawked at the display and spoke excitedly.

Lucas heard the word "kaleidoscope" and guessed at the meaning. He wished he'd paid more attention during the dead languages class at university. He understood a few words she said, like "lovely" and "circle," and he could often determine the general meaning of a statement, but he knew much was lost.

The jump alarm sounded.

Rachel glanced about with concern in her eyes.

Despite his impending queasiness, Lucas smiled. "It'll be fine. Relax. Breathe." He took a deep breath to show her as nausea swept over him.

Rachel's eyes widened, but she seemed to take it better than he did.

The swirling colors in the holoview dissolved into the image of a distant star. The bluish-green planet of Brittany disappeared in the yellow glow of its sun, but he pointed anyway. "We should arrive at the space dock orbiting Brittany soon."

He knew she understood little, but he smiled, and she smiled back.

Military communications were encrypted, but Lucas thought Rachel might like to hear commercial ship-to-ship transmissions of Brittany vessel traffic control. However, when he made the proper adjustments to connect to the ship's ethercomm, the routine and orderly chatter of a busy port didn't come from the device. Instead he heard overlapping panicky voices.

"…Daedalus has been hit… jump… venting atmosphere… fire… breech… assist… orbit decaying… burning up…"

Rachel looked at him with confusion.

Lucas listened with growing apprehension.

Battle stations sounded.

A voice boomed over the vox system. "All hands to battle stations. Brittany is under attack."

Chapter 7

Aboard the HMS Argonaut
Near the Brittany star system

Lucas jumped from his seat. "I've got to go."

Rachel pushed up from her chair.

"No." He held up his palm. "You stay here. If need be, I'll come back for you, but stay… stay here. Okay?"

"Okay." Rachel sat.

Fear etched her face, but Lucas had to leave. As he rushed into the passageway, he locked eyes with Tybalt.

"Follow me," Tybalt ordered.

Lucas followed him down a passageway of flashing red lights, clanging hatches, and a multitude of sailors and marines.

Tybalt glanced over his shoulder as they jogged toward the marine compartments. "We must put aside our differences for now. We have a duty. We are the point of the sword."

Lucas nodded. "We are the point of the sword, Victory our only…" His words trailed off in worry, doubt, and a general lack of *espirt de corps*.

As they continued along the passageway, the jump alarm sounded.

This would be a short jump to Brittany and battle. Bracing himself for the nausea, Lucas slowed his pace. The distortion of space and time hit him as it always did, like a punch in the gut. *Five percent…only five percent of people react this way when a ship jumps. Why do I have to be one of them?*

Tybalt raced ahead.

The queasiness passed within seconds, and Lucas sprinted down the steps of the ladder. Then he rushed aft to the marine operations center. As Lucas expected, Tybalt had taken the command station near the rear of the room. A chair swiveled behind him, but Lucas had never seen Tybalt use it.

An arc of sensor and communications stations stood before Tybalt. Marines stared at displays and communicated with sailors on the bridge to compile the data for the holo display that grew in the center of the room.

Minutes later, the jump alarm sounded again and they returned to normal space near Brittany. As Lucas breathed deep, the planet appeared in the holo display as a blue, green, and brown orb of oceans and continents. Clouds and polar regions provided white accents. Dozens of vessels orbited the planet. Detectors had already identified most as friendly.

Usually the space lift, hanging above the equator and connected only by thin wires to the world below, came under early attack. However, the Brittany space lift appeared untouched and ignored.

The friendly ships were mostly freighters, frigates, and a few yachts. The enemy vessels, while fewer, were all massive ships of the line. From their position about 5,000 miles above the orbiting naval base, they hovered out of effective range of its guns.

Like a silvery moon, the base orbited high above Brittany. The docking loop that girded the base resembled the rings that encircled some planets, but unlike a planet, the ring connected to the base by four spokes. Normally, several ships would have docked along the circle, but Lucas saw none there now.

"Why aren't the Valac attacking the naval base?" Lucas looked to Tybalt for an answer.

Tybalt shook his head. "They're firing at ships' engines—but why?"

Lucas didn't know either.

A young marine pointed to the holo display. "What's that?"

Lucas squinted. A cloud of tiny dots raced around the planet at great speed.

"Are those Valac wasps?" Lucas asked.

Tybalt stepped closer and nodded. "Yes, a huge swarm of them."

Lucas swallowed as fear boiled within. Hundreds of small enemy ships designed for speed and maneuverability would soon fire at them. With wings that allowed atmospheric flight, missile launchers beneath, and a slender nose, they looked more like vicious birds of prey than the wasps of old Earth.

A few carried Valac pilots, but most were unmanned. Fewer still carried Valac marines, trained to board and seize a ship. Lucas shuddered at the thought.

A holo image of Commander Marin appeared beside Tybalt. "Prince Draven is on the orbiting naval station. The Valac are firing on civilian ships that attempt to jump away from the base. We have been ordered to provide cover fire while his yacht escapes."

Lucas focused on the holo image looking for the royal yacht. As the son of a marcher lord, Lucas had met the prince on several occasions. He wished him no harm, but he had no desire to die protecting the second in line to the throne. Yet, as a cadet, he had no voice in the matter. Commander Marin wasn't even consulting Tybalt, just informing.

As the image of the commander dissolved, the ship's engines roared, and her forward velocity exceeded the capacity of the inertia dampers. Lucas stumbled aft several steps but quickly regained his balance. Like an old man walking up a steep hill, he moved toward the holoview.

Sailors on the bridge would navigate the ship, fire the Argonaut guns, and launch the missiles, not marines. Lucas wondered what, if any part he would play in the battle ahead.

As his ship raced closer, various other vessels that had first appeared as dots resolved into complete images. Even without the flags and other technical data displayed in the holoview by the detectors, Lucas could identify several.

A Terran frigate fired on a Valac battleship. He cringed. Brave of the Terran captain, but futile.

Farther away, a civilian freighter maneuvered to escape the fray.

"Katherine?"

At the sound of Tybalt's voice, Lucas glanced to him and then followed his gaze back to the holoview. There, amid all the other ships, he spotted a small civilian ship emblazoned with the Baldwin family crest, but Lucas didn't recognize the craft. He looked at Tybalt, whose eyes remained fixed on the image.

Turning back to the holo display, Lucas hoped his sister was on the planet, not the ship.

"Is that the ship with Prince Draven?" a corporal asked.

From the far side of the base, a civilian ship sped away. The holoview soon displayed the engine type, current velocity, bearing and, finally, the crest of the royal family above the ship.

"Yes," Tybalt said without emotion.

There goes the… Lucas hunted for the right word to describe the prince. *Poltroon?* There were rumors. *Libertine?* There was ample evidence.

The Argonaut guns fired. Missiles whooshed as they launched.

The holoview display now moved in a high-speed dance of objects. Lucas struggled to watch both the royal yacht and the ship his sister was almost certainly aboard.

The naval base slid from the right side of the display to the left while the two Terran frigates moved as one in the opposite direction. The royal yacht shot with ever increasing speed to the right of the display as the Argonaut moved on an intercept course.

The tiny ship that might hold his sister would soon move out of view. He had rarely prayed to the God of Earth, and he never prayed to the Mage, as many commoners did, but the sight of the ship tempted him to pray to both. *Please God, keep Katherine safe.*

The cloud of enemy wasps swarmed past the lead Valac ship.

Lucas didn't have much battle experience, but with the number of enemy wasps and ships, this didn't look like a battle they could win.

And keep me safe, too.

As if punctuating his thoughts, an explosion blasted away the bridge of the nearest Terran ship. It rolled and then drifted out of position.

The Valac wasps ignored it and concentrated their fire on the remaining frigate. The Argonaut engines roared as it raced toward Draven's ship.

Rapid fire seemed to come from every vessel. Missiles reduced numerous wasp fighters into shards of metal, but the Valac pressed their attack. Swarming a frigate, the wasps fired until a mighty explosion filled the display. When it cleared, nothing but hurtling rubble remained of the second Terran frigate.

The only remaining fighting ship was the Argonaut. Wasps and wreckage flew toward them.

Draven's yacht gained speed. Lucas prayed it would jump away so his ship could follow.

The naval base was now a distant object. Lucas struggled to find Katherine's ship but couldn't.

The Argonaut guns continued to blast away at a rapid pace.

The first wasp fired on the royal yacht.

The slower Valac battleships closed to within a thousand miles and fired on the Argonaut.

A Valac missile pierced the defensive fire and slammed into the magshield. The Argonaut rumbled.

Pings and thuds resounded through the vessel as rubble crashed against the shield and ship.

Missiles crisscrossed the display like lightning bolts and crashed into the magshield. Every gun and missile of the Argonaut fired on advancing Valac wasps.

Lucas gasped as the horde of enemy vessels raced away from both the naval base and the Argonaut toward the royal yacht. Despite staggering losses, the wasps continued to streak past.

Explosions rocked the yacht, and it spun out of control. An orange ball of flame enveloped the yacht, but a single escape pod emerged from the blast.

The pod and the Argonaut raced toward each other, closing the thousands of miles between them in seconds. Certain the prince was aboard, Lucas grinned as the magnetic grapplers of the Argonaut latched onto the pod. *Prince Draven is having a rough ride.*

Momentum carried the Argonaut out of view of the naval base. Only the starry heavens now lay before the Argonaut.

"Shift to aft view," Tybalt ordered.

Behind them, a silvery mist of enemy vessels followed. A larger dot, the prince's escape pod, slowly pulled to the Argonaut locked in the magnetic grapplers' field.

Lucas expected to hear the jump alarm any second, but it didn't sound.

The naval base now appeared as just a bright star above the disk of Brittany. Mage Tunnels formed like multi-colored dots against the star-studded blackness. Lucas prayed to the God of Earth that one of them had carried his little sister to safety.

Valac ships and wasps swept in a wide arc away from the orbiting facility. Lucas smiled. "The Valac are moving away from our base."

Tybalt studied the holo image carefully. "Yes. Because, all of them are turning to attack us.".

Chapter 8

Aboard the HMS Argonaut
In the Brittany star system

Once again Commander Marin appeared beside Tybalt. "Prince Draven is onboard at docking bay seven."

A cheer rose in the compartment.

Lucas remained stoic. He glanced at Tybalt who also maintained a somber expression.

"Enemy ships are closing fast," Marin continued. "I need a squad of marines to the bay in case the Valac attempt to board this vessel. When you find Prince Draven, escort him to the bridge. I've ordered the airtight doors between you and the docking bay opened."

Tybalt pointed to Lucas. "Take first squad. Go."

Lucas tapped the communications tech on his shoulder. "Call the squad to the staging area just outside the operations center." As Lucas left the compartment he heard Tybalt ask, "Will we jump soon?"

Commander Marin replied, "We just arrived at this location. The old engines are straining to recharge. I don't believe we'll be able to jump before wasps come within range."

Silently, Lucas cursed their misfortune. In the staging area, just outside of ops, Lucas turned to brief the squad on their mission.

The marines listened intently, apparently excited by the prospect of aiding the prince.

"Let's move," Lucas said with more enthusiasm than he felt.

*   *   *

Rachel relaxed when they turned off the alarm. She didn't know what it had signified, but it certainly sounded like trouble. Now that it stopped, whatever went wrong was probably fixed.

Returning her gaze to the 3D display she'd been watching with Lucas, Rachel noticed beams of light flash from one ship to another. Tiny dots flew back and forth between vessels and seemed to result in explosions.

She'd never been a science fiction fan, but she'd seen a few movies. Using those memories as a guide, she guessed this was a battle, but was it real? She continued to watch and pray that it was just some sort of entertainment.

A dot whizzed toward her.

She flinched.

The ship rumbled and shook.

Pings and bangs reverberated around her.

Rachel stumbled backward. It was all real. She ran from the room and banged on Lucas's door. When no one answered, she tried the knob. It opened. The configuration of his compartment matched her room and stood empty.

Another thunderous roar, and accompanying tremors, sent her running. She sprinted along the passageway and turned a corner in time to see a door twenty feet ahead swing open. She paused. It had opened on its own. A boom from behind convinced her to run through it. Up ahead, a hatch swung open.

Other doors and hatches opened as she ran toward them. The rumble and roar lessened. This must be the direction to safety.

Rachel hurried into the largest compartment she had yet seen. Larger than two gymnasiums, it held craft of several different designs along the two long walls. They could've been spacecraft from a movie set, but this was no movie. Everything, from the monsters to this ship, was real.

She stepped forward, marveling at all the little ships within this big one. The sound of a motor whirred from the far end of the compartment.

Rachel walked toward it.

The device looked something like the ball-return mechanism at a bowling alley, but this one could carry a twenty-foot diameter sphere. The belt crept forward with a single large ball.

Rachel stopped about forty feet away, wondering if the round thing might be some sort of craft.

When the device stopped, mechanical arms grasped the pod.

A family crest had been etched into the craft right above a circular hatch. The hatch clanked open. A dark-haired man only a few years older than her stumbled from the round ship and fell to his hands and knees.

After several dry heaves, he wiped his pale face, smoothed his hair, and stood on shaky legs. He wore a uniform similar to that of Lucas, but this one had more braid and gold and appeared more finely-tailored.

The man locked eyes on Rachel and shouted something in a commanding voice.

She didn't understand and stared at him, confused.

A loud, metallic clang reverberated through the compartment.

He looked toward the sound.

Rachel followed his gaze.

Another loud bang sounded.

Two molten red circles formed on the ceiling near where she'd entered. Rachel pointed to them and turned back to the young man.

His eyes, fixed on the circles, filled with terror. He stumbled backward toward the round ship.

Another bang came from above.

His jaw dropped, and his eyes widened.

Something about the ovals terrified him—but what?

A red hot circle of metal fell to the deck with a clang and then another.

Out of the first two holes poured huge, scorpion-like creatures.

The young man screamed like a little girl.

Rachel wanted to scream. She'd seen the scorpions back on the planet. She'd seen their tails swaying over them and firing stingers like a gun. Running in terror, she had witnessed many of the centipedes die when struck by stingers or torn apart by the mandibles of the scorpions.

Rachel didn't care that the scorpions had killed the centipedes. They had tortured her for days. However, when most of the centipedes were dead, the scorpions came for her. They'd never fired their stingers in her direction, but they chased her, clicking and thrusting their mandibles. She had no desire to be caught.

That time she had run and hid, praying for someone to come and rescue her from the nightmare. Now the nightmare was real and happening again.

The young man reached into the ball ship and pulled out what looked like a rifle. He fumbled with it and fired.

Something impacted near Rachel, but nowhere near the scorpions.

Again he fired at the two advancing groups, but he hit nothing.

She moved closer to him but didn't feel any safer.

Wide-eyed, he continued to fire erratically and only rarely hit the scorpion monsters.

Rachel only heard the clicking of the mandibles and the blast of the gun. Terrified, she stepped back.

Shaking, the young man dropped the weapon and stumbled back.

With their tails arching over their bodies, the scorpions marched closer.

Rachel picked up the weapon. Her father had shown her how to use a gun, but she had little idea how to use this weapon. Still, the cowering guy had used it, so it couldn't be that complicated. She pulled the trigger.

Bang!

The gun slapped her shoulder.

Something impacted near the eye of a monster. Greenish goo oozed from the spot, but the thing kept moving.

The guy hid behind her, like a frightened toddler, and mumbled.

She fired again.

The scorpion dropped to the floor, but others hurried toward her.

As fast as she could, Rachel shot at another.

Chapter 9

Aboard the HMS Argonaut in the Brittany star system

Crouching behind a tool cart, Lucas used the ether-comm on his sleeve to report in. "The hull in the launch bay has been breached." His heart pounded, and his voice rasped against his dry throat. "Valac have entered the compartment through three holes. There are about…." He glanced over the cart. "I see about twenty. A few are dead or wounded. We're pushing forward."

He ran along the wing of a nearby dart to better cover. Valac stingers slammed into the hull inches from his face.

The bang and thud of lance fire, the clicking of mandibles and the whoosh of aculeus stingers filled his ears. Marines on both sides of him fired on advancing Valac.

From his sleeve screen came Tybalt's voice. "Do you see the prince?"

"No, but someone is shooting at the far end of the compartment."

"Hopefully that's Prince Draven. Get to him quickly."

"Yes, sir."

Aiming at a nearby Valac, Lucas fired and sprinted to another position. He climbed onto the wing of another dart. Ten Valac formed a defensive line ahead of them, but the remainder kept advancing on the far end of the compartment. He relayed the information to Tybalt.

"I'm coming with the rest of the marines," Tybalt announced. The screen went blank.

Lucas shouted to a nearby corporal. "Take five men and run to the far side. The rest of us will provide cover fire."

He climbed to a higher viewpoint for better shooting. Peeking over the top of the craft, he observed a semi-circle of Valac around an escape pod with the royal insignia. Then he spotted Prince Draven crawling on his hands and knees toward the pod and away from a guard.

The guard fired rapidly at the oncoming Valac. Lucas squinted. The guard wore a baggy marine uniform but had straight blonde hair that hung down to his chest, much longer than regulation allowed.

He fumbled for his bioculus. As the image came into focus he saw not a guard, and not even a man, but Rachel. His heart pounded. *How did she get here?* He wanted to race to her but, at the moment such an act would be suicide. He shouted the location of the prince to the Marines and fired on the Valac nearest to Rachel.

As Lucas watched and fired, Prince Draven disappeared into the pod. When Lucas next spotted the prince, he stood in the hatchway holding a lance, but not firing. Terror radiated from his face. A few feet away, Rachel shot at the Valac with impressive speed and accuracy.

A familiar nausea swept through Lucas. The Argonaut had jumped.

*   *   *

As Rachel continued to fire, a strange sensation swept over her. She had experienced it once before with Lucas. He'd indicated that she shouldn't worry about it. Despite their inauspicious first meeting, she'd grown to trust Lucas, so she pushed the fading feeling from her mind and fired again.

No matter how fast she fired, the scorpion-like monsters kept getting closer. She shot again.

Another monster collapsed to the floor.

Bang.

Thud.

As they circled around her they bunched together making shooting them easy.

She fired again.

Another one dropped, but others drew within only fifteen feet of her position. Rachel heard shooting in the distance, but without help right there with her, the monsters would soon close in and tear her to pieces.

She glanced behind her. The terrified guy crawled on the floor. *No help there.*

Bang.

She fired and fired again, but they kept coming.

She shot a scorpion on her left, and then one to her right collapsed.

With a quick glance in that direction, she spotted Lucas on top of one of the smaller ships.

The monsters closed to within ten feet, but, with new hope, she continued shooting.

Something moved in her peripheral vision. She swung to her left. A scorpion loomed so close she could touch it. She screamed.

From somewhere within the monster came a strange, almost Asian melody. Some notes of the song resonated so high that they hurt her ears, and others resounded so low she felt the waves rumble through her.

Confused, she still managed to pull the trigger, but the gun didn't fire. Panic filled her. She dropped the weapon and stumbled backward.

The scorpion continued to sing.

Thud.

Green fluid flowed from a hole in the monster's head.

The song stopped as the scorpion slumped to the floor.

Twenty yards away, Lucas continued to fire on nearby monsters.

Rachel turned toward the pod in search of another weapon. The guy had retreated to the pod. He stood in the hatch with wide terrified eyes—and another gun. She grabbed it and continued to shoot.

Seconds later, she spotted a half-dozen other soldiers firing on the scorpions. The monsters shot back at the soldiers, but not at her. She didn't know why and didn't have time to think about it.

The cowardly guy picked up the empty gun, fiddled with something, pointed, and shot.

Huh? It wasn't empty? She fired her new weapon again.

The soldiers shot from several vantage points. Six monsters returned fire on the soldiers. A seventh turned toward Rachel and the guy beside her.

The scorpion lunged and slid to a stop only a few feet from her.

The coward screamed, fell to his knees, and fired.

For a moment Rachel again heard the strange melody. Then the song died, and the scorpion slumped to the ground.

As she searched for another target, Rachel wilted to the floor, exhausted.

*   *   *

Since the Argonaut had jumped, only a few Valac, still alive and onboard, threatened the ship. He fired at one and then heard a human scream. He swept around in time to see Prince Draven shoot a Valac inches from Rachel.

She collapsed to her knees.

Lucas killed the last Valac between them and dashed to Rachel's side. "Are you hurt?"

She pulled her long blonde hair from her face and smiled at him.

As Lucas helped her stand, he stared into her eyes. He'd heard of women fighting alongside men in the early days of Terra, but those were legendary tales. Today he'd witnessed both courage and beauty wrapped in one body.

With difficulty, he tore his gaze from her and looked about. All the Valac lay dead, and the medicus worked with the wounded marines.

He turned to the prince. Normally he'd bow, but he stood before the prince in uniform and, while the army might salute everywhere, the navy and marines didn't salute aboard the ship. "Uh... your Royal Highness, I've been ordered to escort you to the bridge."

"Belay that, Cadet."

Lucas turned. A dozen marines jogged toward him with Tybalt in the lead.

"I will escort you to the bridge, Your Highness," Tybalt nodded. "I'm Lieutenant Archer, senior marine officer on the Argonaut."

"Thank you, Lieutenant." Prince Draven handed his weapon to Lucas and squinted at him. "Do I know you?"

"Yes, Your Highness. I am Lord Lucas Baldwin, son of the Marquis of Devon."

"Ah, yes." The prince wagged his finger. "You're Victor's younger brother. Fine soldier, that one. You have much to live up to."

"Yes, Your Highness," Lucas said flatly.

The prince looked Rachel up and down. "And do we now have women in the corps of marines?"

Both Tybalt and Lucas quickly said no.

"She's just a commoner, Your Highness. We saved her from the Valac during an earlier battle, and she needed clothing." With a serious look on his face, Tybalt turned to Lucas. "Take the woman to her quarters. This encounter with Valac must have distressed her greatly."

"Yes, sir." Lucas gestured toward Rachel. "Follow me."

"Shall we go, Your Highness?" Tybalt asked.

The prince ran a hand through his longish, dark-hair. "Very well, let's leave this place."

Guiding Rachel by the arm, Lucas led her toward a side hatch. Such closeness might cause some gossip among the marines, but that wasn't his main concern. The longer Rachel spent in Prince Draven's presence, the more likely she would speak and pose questions for which Lucas had few answers.

As they exited the landing bay, Lucas felt a weight slide from him. This would serve as his second combat mission of record, and this time he had encountered live Valac on a battlefield. He leaned against the bulkhead and breathed deeply.

I fought the Valac in battle. I did my duty… I'm not a coward. He smiled. *I'm a marine… I'm a man and I'm alive!*

*   *   *

As they neared the hatch, Rachel looked over her shoulder at the monsters now dead on the floor. She had no idea what they were or why they seemed to sing to her.

A few feet beyond the hatch, Lucas leaned against the wall and breathed deeply.

Rachel grinned as a smile spread slowly across Lucas' face.

She stood beside him and squeezed his hand while hoping that some of his smile was for her. "I wish I could speak your language."

A lot she didn't understand, but Lucas was brave and cared for her. For now, that would be enough.

Chapter 10

Aboard the HMS Argonaut
Near the Brittany star system

Lucas certainly didn't want Rachel to start talking about Earth in front of Prince Draven, so they waited in a side passage. She leaned her head on Lucas's shoulder, apparently content to just be there with him.

Finally he heard movement and peeked around the corner. Tybalt, the prince, and most of the marines strode down the passageway.

Rachel maintained a strong grip on his hand as they hurried toward the berthing area. From her tone and words like, "monster" and "scorpion," he could tell she asked many questions. He knew she'd asked about the Valac, but couldn't fathom a way to discuss the aliens or the war using the few words they mutually understood. Again, he vowed to learn English.

She leaned into him, said something, and smiled.

He couldn't deny the feelings they seemed to share, but he imagined presenting her back home.

Father, may I introduce Rachel. I don't know her family name. She fights like a man and might be crazy. I doubt it, but she could be. She most definitely killed an Aux and is probably a commoner.

The idea that his infatuation might cause her pain stabbed at his heart. However, thoughts of family brought his mind back to Katherine. Again he prayed to the God of Earth that she had survived the battle and jumped away.

Sailors in biohazard gear jogged down the passageway. They would have the unpleasant job of cleaning the launch bay and removing bodies and blood, both alien and human.

Leading Rachel, he hurried in the opposite direction. When they reached her berthing, Rachel waved him in.

"No, I can't. I still have duties. Please, this time, stay."

"I will stay."

He still heard her strange accent, but he wondered if he might've grown more accustomed to it and thereby understood more words.

"Good," he said more emphatically than he intended. As he jogged toward the bridge, his thoughts lingered back at her room. He'd be glad when they could truly converse. He wanted to share more with her.

Now that both the ship and prince were safe, the squad of marines that accompanied Tybalt stood in the passageway engaged in idle conversation.

Lucas walked past them onto the bridge. Technicians feverishly worked the consoles along the bulkheads. Captain Marin, Tybalt, and the prince stood near the holoview. Reluctant to join, Lucas stopped several feet away.

"Why did the Valac shoot only at the engines?" Prince Draven asked.

Captain Marin rubbed his chin. "I suspect they wanted to stop us, not destroy us."

Draven stiffened, his eyes wide. "To what end?"

"Perhaps your capture." Tybalt said. "The progress of the attack would suggest such a plan."

The captain nodded.

Prince Draven's eyes widened.

Lucas decided to approach, be brief and, if possible, leave quickly. He moved into their line of sight and came to attention.

The captain nodded.

"Your Highness, Captain, and sir, the female has been returned to her quarters." He glanced at Tybalt and asked, "Shall I take first squad back to the operations center?"

Tybalt looked to the captain with a raised brow.

The captain pursed his lips. "This jump is short. Less than three Gellers. I prefer to keep the marines close to Prince Draven until we know the situation at Brittany." He turned to a technician. "When will we return to normal space?"

The technician gazed at the display. "We're near the end of the Mage Tunnel. Sixty seconds from... now. Shall I sound the alarm?"

The captain nodded. "Yes, at once."

Lips taunt and neck muscles tight, the prince stared at the holoview.

Lucas braced himself for the inevitable nausea as the alarm sounded.

Moments later, the swirl of colors and sparkles changed into the blackness of deep space. At this distance Brittany's yellow star appeared as just one faint dot, among many.

The captain and the prince discussed what to do next. "As soon as we establish long range communications, we should send a message that you're safe."

The prince nodded.

"Then we can take you wherever you wish."

"LRC established," the communications technician announced. "We've received the all-clear signal from Brittany."

A murmur of approval spread across the bridge.

"All clear? What a shame." The prince smirked. "I had hoped to kill more Valac today."

Tybalt motioned with his head for Lucas to follow him. Together they retreated to a quiet corner of the bridge.

"Prince Draven has asked me several questions about Rachel. He told the captain she killed one of the Valac."

"She killed more than one." Lucas described what he'd seen in the docking bay.

Tybalt's gaze flitted between the captain and Draven. "We need to get Rachel off this ship as soon as possible. If Katherine is still at Brittany and she's okay, perhaps you could get Rachel—"

Lucas shook his head. "I'm reluctant to get Katherine involved."

"Our plan was to travel on your family yacht—with Katherine. How would that not involve her?"

Lucas frowned. "It appears that earlier I thought only of myself. Now I'm considering the consequences of our actions and do not wish to involve my little sister."

Tybalt shook his head. "Such noble inaction may not be possible."

The captain called for Tybalt to join him at the holoview.

"Yes, sir. Tybalt turned back to Lucas and whispered, "If you can, devise another plan—quickly."

Lucas stood back, still hoping to soon leave the compartment. He overheard the Prince Draven thank the captain for something, and then the prince stepped away, casually observing the sailors on the bridge with an air of confident authority.

The captain turned to Tybalt. "I wanted to let you know we'll jump back to Brittany as soon as the engines recharge. Elements of the Orion Fleet have arrived in the system and more are expected soon. When we return, the prince will transfer to the Admiral's flagship."

Tybalt nodded at the prince just a few feet away. "An excellent plan."

The captain faced Tybalt. "The cadet and first squad are dismissed."

The prince stepped close to both Lieutenant Archer and the captain. "However, before I go, I wish to speak privately with that young lady who fought beside me."

Chapter 11

Aboard the HMS Argonaut
Near the Brittany star system

Lucas hurried from the bridge when he heard the royal request to speak with Rachel. It might have been said politely, the prince even smiled as he spoke, but it amounted to a royal command.

Lucas was not about to help Draven, but needed time to devise a plan to keep him and Rachel apart.

The jump engines had most likely completely discharged and would need time to recharge. When they jumped, the Argonaut would proceed to the edge of the star system and then coordinate the short jump to the planet with the Port Master at traffic control. Unfortunately, the old engines and jump protocols gave the prince more time to meet with Rachel.

Lucas prayed he would soon confirm his sister's safety, but more pressing was how to keep Rachel away from the prince. Still lacking a strategy, Lucas hurried to officer berthing and knocked on Rachel's door with only a vague plan in mind.

Rachel swung open the door.

Without entering, Lucas took her by the hand. "Come with me."

She didn't resist as Lucas hurried her away.

Fortunately, most of the crew remained on station, not walking the passageways. Lucas led her down three levels to a gray deck lined with conduit and pipes without encountering another crewman. He wasn't sure if the sweat that beaded on his forehead came from the temperature or his own worry.

Finally, they arrived at the hatch to the helot quarters. He looked down the dark hole—the very one he'd refused to go through with Tybalt mere hours earlier.

He knew that hiding a woman from the prince wasn't treason. Indeed, he felt good about it, but daring to believe Rachel came from Earth and questioning the truth of history as revealed by the Mage and taught in all the Kingdoms of Terra—*that* was treason.

As he stepped on the first rung of the ladder, he looked back at Rachel. "Come with me, please." He released her hand.

Her grin appeared forced.

Perhaps she'd never used a ladder. Such devices were certainly easier to use wearing uniform pants, as she did, than the normal dress of a woman. However, once she started, she proceeded down with ease and jumped off two rungs from the bottom.

Usually lights came on when entering a room, but all remained shrouded in darkness. He'd never ventured into this part of the ship, but he'd banged his head on enough pipes and tripped over enough hatch frames to warrant caution. Gradually, his eyes adjusted, and a compartment of gray and black came into view.

Up ahead, a hatch creaked open allowing a dim yellow glow to cast long shadows down the passageway. He wasn't sure who or what was up ahead, but enough light entered the compartment to allow safe movement. Having no better plan, he led Rachel toward the light as the beat of his heart thundered in his ears.

Lucas led her into the next compartment which amounted to little more than a wide spot in the passageway. A dozen hammocks lined the bulkheads on either side of the uncomfortably warm, dimly lit space. Six helots wearing only their linen tunics emerged from the darkness and formed a semi-circle before him, but said nothing.

Lucas grasped Rachel's hand as he searched for the right words to say to the helots.

A gray-haired man walked from the far end of the compartment into the light. He wiped his face with a tattered rag. "Lieutenant Tybalt visited us earlier."

"I am officer cadet—"

The old man waved a hand. "We know who you are, Lord Lucas, son of Farold Baldwin, Marques of Devon and—"

"You know the names and titles of my family, but you do not know me." Lucas glowered at him.

The older man looked carefully at Lucas and then at Rachel. "Perhaps I don't. Is this the young lady from Earth?"

Lucas hadn't thought about what he'd say and was reluctant to reveal the fact of his treason to helots but they apparently already knew. With more confidence in his voice than in his heart, he declared, "Yes, this is Rachel of Earth."

All the helots bowed to Rachel, and Lucas again wondered about the wisdom of his present course of action.

The gray-haired man again looked Lucas in the eye. "Sir Tybalt told us you might bring her to us." He turned to his fellow helots. "I will speak with Lord Lucas and the Daughter of Earth alone."

The others again bowed to Rachel and left through a nearby hatch.

"My name is Konrad." The gray-haired man gestured to three crates along the bulkhead. He moved one box to a better position and sat.

Lucas sat across from Konrad.

After moving her crate close to Lucas, Rachel sat.

Konrad spoke first. "I am an elder among the Seekers of Earth on this ship."

"Seekers of Earth" was how the helots often referred to themselves, but the phrase had been outlawed by royal decree. Konrad had committed a crime in using it, and if Lucas didn't report him, he would also transgress the law.

I'm compiling a significant criminal record today. He sighed inwardly.

Konrad gazed at Rachel and then Lucas. "What do you need from us?"

Briefly, Lucas explained that he wished to keep Rachel hidden from Prince Draven until he left the ship."

"From what I am told, most ladies of virtue wish to remain hidden from the prince."

Lucas smiled at the comment and wondered where these helots had learned such news. "Do any seekers speak English?" he asked.

"Teaching English to one of us is a crime."

"So is referring to your people as seekers—Seeker Konrad."

The elder smiled. "Most speak only lingua Terra, but a few of us know English."

"Good." Lucas stood and Konrad did also.

Rachel remained seated, but her eyes darted between the two.

Lucas smiled gently. "Do your best to protect her."

Konrad turned to Rachel. "We have all pledged our lives to protect the Daughter of Earth."

Lucas cast him a questioning glance. "Daughter of Earth. Bowing. There's more here than I understand."

Konrad smiled. "Yes, there is. I don't know if it's a prophecy or a hope or if such a prophecy is also a hope for the future, but it has long been said that God would send a daughter of Earth to lead us out of bondage."

"The God of Earth would send someone?"

"There is only one God."

Lucas hoped his smile didn't display the disdain he felt. "I must go before I'm missed." He turned to Rachel, but he meant his words for both. "Be careful."

Fear spread across her face.

Lucas bent over and gently grasped her hand. "You will be safe here." *I hope.* "I'll return shortly."

Konrad spoke softly to Rachel.

Rachel gasped.

English. Konrad had spoken English. Lucas stared at him. "What did you say?"

Konrad turned to Lucas. "I told her what you said." He called for another helot to climb the ladder to the main passageway while Rachel and Konrad continued to talk.

The man at the top of the ladder reported the way clear.

"Thank you." Reluctantly, Lucas departed. As he hurried down the passageway, he realized today marked the first time he had ever thanked a helot.

The profanation "helot" rolled around in his mind as he jogged toward the marine compartments. He would need to continue using the term, but it already sounded wrong to him.

Reaching his destination, Lucas peeked around the corner into the operations center. A dozen techs sat inside. Casually he slipped by and into the enlisted berthing area. The compartment Lucas shared with Tybalt felt cramped, but in the enlisted berthing areas bunks were stacked three high in long rows. Everything these marines owned fit into one tiny gray locker next to their bunk.

Lucas saw a marine he recalled from the fight in the docking bay. "Private, I saw you kill a Valac during the fight. Was that your first?"

"Yes, sir."

"Excellent. I'll be sure to put that in my report. Who else killed one?"

Many hands shot into the air.

For several minutes he patted the men on the back, congratulated others, and made sure everyone would remember that he'd been there.

As he talked, the jump alarm sounded. Lucas continued to speak and smile even when the familiar wave of nausea swept over him and passed. He commended a marine for two kills and then moved on.

Walking into the storage compartment, Lucas spotted another marine from the fight and started a conversation with him. *I should move on to the operations center before someone comes looking for me.*

He turned but movement and murmur at the far end of the storage area caught his attention.

Several dozen marines split to form a lane for Tybalt to approach. Behind him, Prince Draven talked with several of the men.

"Cadet Baldwin," Tybalt said in a firm voice. "Prince Draven and I have been looking for you."

Chapter 12

Aboard the HMS Argonaut
Near the Brittany star system

"I've been here, sir."

The marines around him nodded.

"What do you need, sir?"

"Where is the girl, Rachel?" Tybalt's face and voice remained stern.

"I returned her to her berth as you ordered, sir."

"She isn't there. I need you to find her promptly."

"Yes, sir." *Stall. I've got to stall for time.*

Lucas turned to launch his faux search then paused. "Could we use internal sensors?"

Prince Draven smiled. "Excellent idea."

Tybalt shook his head. "They can't tell a man from a woman."

Lucas tried to think of something else that would sound useful. "Have we checked the vids?"

On this old ship, none operated near officer berthing or on the lower decks near the helot compartments.

"Yes." Tybalt rubbed his chin. "They didn't show her."

Lucas tried to think of something else but couldn't. "I'll begin my search. Excuse me, Your Highness."

"You should send others to search for her," Prince Draven said to Tybalt.

"Yes, of course. I'll have my men search this compartment and the passageways. I believe the captain already has sailors checking their work areas and spaces.

Lucas nodded. "I'll check her berthing and other places I know she has visited." He hoped that Konrad would keep her in the helot berthing area.

"We will find her, Your Highness," Tybalt asserted.

Glancing down every passage and checking around corners, Lucas walked fast enough to avoid suspicion, but no faster. If anyone checked the vids later he wanted it to appear that he really searched.

After an inevitably fruitless search of both her berth and his, Lucas stood in the passageway and he tried to think where he would go if he truly looked for the girl. He decided to check the brig, the only other area of the ship that she knew. Of course that compartment connected to the Master-at-arms space, so it seemed unlikely she would remain unnoticed, but it still seemed logical to check.

When he opened the door to the brig compartment a lone sailor sat behind a desk in the tiny office.

"We're looking for the woman that's onboard."

The sailor shook his head. "So I've heard, sir. She isn't here."

As he turned Lucas came face-to-face with Chief Sadler.

"Why do you think she'd be here, cadet?" the master-at-arms chief asked.

His mind blank and his mouth dry, Lucas worked to form an answer for the ship's law enforcement officer. "Uh... I don't, but it was one of the few places on the ship she's familiar with."

Sadler nodded. "I suppose that's true. Where have you checked?"

As Lucas described every aspect of his quasi search the jump alarm sounded. Despite the nausea that he knew would come, he smiled inwardly and continued his discussion with the master-at-arms.

Seconds later the ship jumped, and Lucas gritted his teeth. "I'll check the wardroom and galley next. The smell of food might have drawn her to either location."

Chief Sadler nodded, and Lucas hurried away from the Master-at-arms.

With the Chief safely out of sight, Lucas slowed to a walk. Every step so far had been an elaborate show in a pretend search. The wardroom would be empty at this time. He decided to check it.

On his way there, he realized the minutes ahead would reveal whether his sister Katherine had reached safety and if Rachel would remain so. His gut knotted in worry.

As expected, the wardroom stood empty. Leaving the vacant compartment, he sighed. Since the hunt had not been called off it seemed logical that no one had found Rachel.

Lucas continued his fake search efforts while pondering the realization that few ever considered the helots, or seekers, as he'd begun to think of them. They existed like ghosts. There, but invisible, and thought of only on occasion. Lucas didn't believe in ghosts and hoped this wouldn't be the rare occasion that someone thought of the helots.

In the main galley, a half-dozen helots and a few frowning sailors toiled in the hot, humid compartment.

"Now where to search next?" he muttered.

* * *

Thrilled that someone spoke English, even with a heavy accent, Rachel had asked Konrad one question after another since Lucas left.

"So the Earth was destroyed?" She shuddered to think her mom, dad, and big brother might be dead.

Konrad shrugged. "That's what most people believe."

"But this is a spaceship, right?" She looked about still trying to comprehend the idea of being in space. "Can't you just go check and see?"

"Space is vast… infinite, actually, and we don't know the location of Earth."

"How long ago did all of this happen? If it did happen."

"We don't know exactly, but around 300 years ago."

"But I've only been awake for a few days. How could the Earth have been destroyed so many years in the past?"

He shook his head. "We have the technology to suspend people in a sleep-like state. It is often used to preserve the life of those seriously injured in battle. It does slow aging, but the longest period I've ever heard of was about a year."

Rachel tried to comprehend that everyone she ever knew had likely died hundreds of years ago. Tears welled in her eyes.

"But I must tell you another story. The story of my people, the Seekers of Earth."

*   *   *

Lucas glanced at the sailors repairing the holes in the docking bay. They'd positioned patches and began pumping liquid steel into the first gap. Returning his gaze to the prince, he tried to look disappointed.

Captain Marin walked toward the group still leaning on a cane. Tybalt followed looking as intense as a man in combat.

Standing at attention in front of Prince Draven, Marin said, "Your Highness, as captain of this vessel I wish to express my personal regret that we failed to locate this troublesome woman."

Draven nodded. "Lord Lucas mentioned the lady might be a lunatic."

The captain relaxed slightly. "Yes. Some of her actions have suggested that."

An alarm sounded, and sailors scurried to clear from the area where the admiral's large, luxurious Sabina-class dart approached on the magrail. When it came to rest nearby, eight sideboys formed up near the ramp and held a salute.

A voice boomed over the ship's vox. "His Royal Highness, Prince Draven, departing."

The prince turned toward the dart and then spun back to face Captain Marin. "I'll be reporting the security breech regarding the woman onboard to the admiral. Still, if you find her and she isn't a lunatic, I would like to speak with her."

The captain's face slumped. "Of course, Your Highness."

The prince boarded the admiral's dart, and within moments it rumbled along a rail to the launch tube and hurtled into the void.

Captain Marin turned to Tybalt and Lucas. "Find that woman, and get her off my ship!"

"Yes, sir," they said in near unison.

The captain Marin sighed and then with a less stern voice continued. "The Valac have taken the mining facility on Bodmin. It appears they plan to use the system for a major offensive in this sector. The Pegasus fleet jumped into battle minutes ago. Lead elements of the Orion fleet will soon follow.

"The Argonaut has orders to wait for the arrival of other marine units and another battlegroup. I don't know exactly when that will be, but I want that woman off my ship before we jump."

"Yes, sir," Tybalt said.

The captain grunted and walked away.

Lucas and Tybalt retreated to a corner of the docking bay.

Tybalt leaned close. "Where did you hide her?"

"With the he—the seekers."

Tybalt cast a wry smile. "So you've met and talked with them."

"Briefly."

"They seem to have made an impression upon you." Tybalt rubbed his chin. "Continue to pretend to look for the girl. I'll contact you when she's back in her quarters. We can say she remained overwrought from the battle, left her compartment, and got lost again, but she found her way back." Tybalt took a deep breath. "Have you formulated a plan other than having Rachel return with your sister to Devon?"

Lucas shook his head.

"Then I suggest we allow Katherine to decide if she wishes to join our conspiracy."

For the next thirty minutes, Lucas pretended to search the forward part of the ship as most of the marines searched the stern. Hopefully, Rachel remained hidden amidships with the Seekers.

Nearing the bridge, he could restrain his anxiety no longer. He entered. The captain stood with his hands clasped behind his back, staring at the holoview.

Lucas avoided his line of sight, but for several moments searched for any sign of his sister in the display. Two Terran dreadnaughts and a command ship orbited Brittany base. A dozen other military vessels orbited high above the planet with still more in low orbit. Freighters circled the space lift over the equator. Darts sped between the ships, base and lift. Everything flowed in a slow dance that made it impossible to isolate and identify one relatively small ship.

He moved close to one of the sensor techs. "I thought I saw one of my family vessels during the battle. I'm worried that my sister may have been caught up in the fight. Would you check to see if she's still here?"

"Yes, sir." The sailor tapped the screen before him with fingers of both hands. Moments later a ship diagram and specifications appeared on the display. "The only vessel registered to the Baldwin family is this Curtana class dart."

Information from the detectors and the registry database scrolled on a large screen above the main workstation.

Lucas stared at the display. Usually, that model and configuration moved high-value freight. No one he knew used them for personal transport. Also, they were frugal compared to the family yacht, not at all like the luxurious comfort of Katherine's usual travels. Hoping his sister had left the system and not died in it, Lucas thanked the sailor and turned away.

"Uh, sir? This ship has been modified." He pointed to the passenger section. "This area has been extended and converted." Then he gestured aft. "Look at those engines."

Most of the cargo area now resembled three staterooms, complete with bathing rooms, water closets, and a separate galley area. With its new engines, the vessel could outrun most ships its size.

Lucas chuckled. The design looked like something his sister would commission, but where did she get the money? He couldn't imagine Father giving it to her.

"What is the ship's name?" he asked.

The technician tapped the screen. "The Lady Katherine."

Subtle, Sis. How she'd gotten the ship would have to wait. Right now he needed a way to get Rachel to his sister's ship, explain to Katherine the situation, and get her cooperation. *One problem at a time.*

Lucas walked from the bridge deep in thought. Then he stopped, returned, and walked up to the captain.

Without looking at him the captain said, "Have you found her?"

"Not yet, sir, but I believe my sister is in the Brittany system."

"So?"

"When I find Rach... uh, the missing woman, I suggest she be taken to my sister's craft." Lucas pointed to it on the holoview. "Someone from my family can see her home."

"Yes. That would be excellent. Just find her and get her off my ship."

"Yes, sir, as soon as she is found, I'll personally escort her off."

The captain gave a nod and grunt.

With all the permission he needed, Lucas hurried from the bridge to contact his sister. He understood the need for military security, but when trying to contact Katherine, such rules stood as an impediment. No human had ever been discovered giving secrets to the Valac, but several had sent messages to family and loved ones that gave away ship positions, so modern military vessels limited personal transmissions. Thus he needed to use the ship-to-ship ethercomm in Tybalt's office. Even if someone asked why he contacted a civilian vessel, he had the orders of the captain as justification.

However, no one paid Lucas any attention as he entered the marine operations center. He preferred it that way. The arc of communications, detector, and intel stations hummed with activity as technicians hurried about.

Tybalt talked with three senior officers via a small holoview beside the command chair. Lucas paused and stood just out of view as Tybalt continued to speak and listen. The officers had just arrived on a command ship. The Argonaut would soon leave as part of the reinforced Orion fleet.

Lucas needed to hurry.

Glancing at the main holoview, Lucas noted that the Argonaut now orbited Brittany base. A line of darts stretched between one of the dreadnaughts and a supply ship. Two others disappeared into Mage Tunnels as he watched.

Continuing on to Tybalt's office, he sat at the either-comm, adjusted the crystals, and connected with The Lady Katherine.

Only as the display resolved the image did he consider what words to say. Care would be needed on the public channel.

"Lucas!" she cried. "What a horrifying battle. I thought I might die. Are you okay? Is Tybalt well?"

"I am well. Tybalt is fine, and I'm glad to see that you're unhurt. However, the battle has changed our plans. Tybalt won't be able to leave the ship."

"But you will?"

"Briefly. I have someone I'd like you to meet."

"You're not working with Father to marry me off are you? I've heard that Prince Draven is in the Brittany system."

"Marry? Draven?" He wanted to shout no, but he recalled being on an open channel. "No, you misunderstand. The young lady is—"

"A woman? How did you meet her? Is she someone of rank?"

"I suppose she's a commoner, but I don't really know."

Katherine frowned. "How did you meet this woman?"

"She came aboard after a recent battle. I'll tell you more in person, but right now I need to get her off the ship before—" He stopped. He'd almost said too much.

She shook her head as she smiled. "Only you and Victor could meet a woman in the midst of combat. Certainly, bring her when you come. I would be pleased to meet your new amour."

Chapter 13

Aboard the HMS Argonaut
In the Brittany star system

Lucas hurried through the landing bay to the adjacent dart operations office. Damage control teams continued patching the Valac burn holes in the hull. No hint of enemy corpses remained.

Inside, the duty officer gave instructions to an approaching supply ship. When he finished, Lucas drew near. "Excuse me, sir. The captain has ordered me to remove the woman from the ship before we jump. I've arranged to take her to a civilian vessel."

The officer nodded. "Captain Marin just advised me. When you're ready, use number seven."

Lucas rushed across the ship to Rachel's berthing. Lucas found her, as promised, sitting in her room. Konrad, the gray-haired seeker, stood beside her.

Panting, Lucas spoke to them both. "I'm going to take Rachel to my sister's ship. Come, we must hurry."

Rachel looked to Konrad.

Lucas waited impatiently as the two spoke in English. *Does everyone know the dead language—except me?*

By Konrad's tone and a few understood words, Lucas determined that Konrad plead for Rachel to go.

"I've told Rachel it would be best to leave with you, but she refuses." Konrad shrugged. "She wants to stay here with... well, me, because I speak her language."

Briefly, Lucas imagined dragging Rachel down the passageway while she kicked and screamed. However, he had no desire to hurt or embarrass her, and he could imagine what his father would say when the gossips spread word of the event.

Rachel spoke again to Konrad, who translated, "She will go, if I go."

"So be it. Konrad, come with us. I'll invent some excuse for your absence after we return."

Rachel stood, and clutched canvas bag with a draw string at the top.

"What's that?" Lucas opened the door.

"Tybalt brought it. He said it was food for the journey."

Lucas shrugged then jogged into the passageway. His sister would certainly have better nourishment than anything on this ship.

With Rachel on his arm, Lucas led and Konrad followed toward the docking bay. As they, entered Rachel clutched his hand and looked about.

He squeezed her hand. "There's nothing to fear. The Valac are gone—and so is Prince Draven." He pointed to Sabre-class dart number seven. With its wings folded back and weapons retracted, it resembled a gently sloping black rectangle. The rear hatch stood open with the ramp down, waiting for them. "Hurry."

They rushed onboard.

"Retract the ramp, and secure the hatch." Lucas dashed to the pilot seat and strapped in.

"Ramp up. Hatch secure," Konrad shouted from the rear.

Lucas glanced over his shoulder and saw Konrad helping Rachel with the seat straps. He adjusted the ethercomm. "Operations, this is dart seven requesting launch."

Clank.

"Sabre seven, you are locked. Standby."

Moments later the craft rumbled along the magrail into the launch tube.

The controller's voice came over the ethercomm, "Sabre seven launch in three, two, one—"

The vessel shot down the tube. The lights along either side blurred into continuous blue lines.

Lucas thrust the throttle forward.

The engines roared to life, and the craft shot away from the Argonaut.

As Lucas made the first turn, Rachel giggled. Looking over his shoulder, he watched as Konrad helped her from the straps, and she floated into the air.

He made a gentle course correction, and Rachel drifted into the bulkhead. Then, as the craft maintained a constant course and speed, he watched Rachel float to the middle, spinning and twirling.

Her eyes widened as she vomited into her mouth, and slapped her hand across it.

Pleased she had that bit of control, he reached into the pilot's locker for a water bottle and tossed it to Konrad.

He showed Rachel how to use it and gave the bottle to her.

She gulped down several mouthfuls as her face grew redder. Seconds later, Rachel swam to Lucas' side and stared out the viewport with wide eyes. Off the starboard, the green and blue orb of Brittany shined. On the port side, one of the dreadnaughts orbited the slowly turning naval base.

Lucas motioned for Rachel to sit in the navigator seat beside him. She did and strapped herself in.

Lucas spotted his sister's ship. "Lady Katherine, this is Argonaut Seven. Prepare for docking."

"Certainly, brother. I'll maintain a constant speed. You come to me."

Lucas smiled. She wanted him to do all the course changes. Did she doubt her skills? He had only seen her pilot on short sub-orbital trips. "Lady Katherine, affirmative, but are you sure you don't want to maneuver to me?"

"Be nice, brother. I did come all this way, and into a battle, for you."

"Affirmative," he smiled. "I'll dock with you in five minutes."

He fired the rockets to slow the craft and descend in orbit. Now moving faster, he gained on his sister's ship.

He aligned their docking ports from behind and matched speed. Now only a thousand yards aft, he fired rockets briefly to close the final distance and engaged the auto-docking controller.

The clang of clamps and a green light confirmed a secure docking. Lucas opened the hatch into the airlock of his sister's ship and grasped the first rung of the ladder. "Both of you stay here, please, until I've explained the situation to Katherine."

Konrad nodded and translated the message for Rachel.

Lucas gently pulled himself up and floated into the ten-foot long tube to The Lady Katherine airlock. As he drifted upward his speed increased. Realizing his weight was returning, he did a flip and grabbed hold of the ladder. Now instead of floating up toward Katherine's ship, he climbed down the ladder toward it.

Standing in the airlock, he shouted to Konrad. "The Lady Katherine has gravity." He turned toward the hatch.

A different-looking Katherine smiled, waved, and opened the airlock door for him.

They shared the same brown eyes and auburn hair, but her features had the tenderness of a lady. Lucas noted that her locks flowed only to shoulder-length, not down to the middle of her back as they had for years. As the daughter of a marcher lord, Katherine usually wore the latest fashion in gowns and dresses, but today she stood before him in a black jumpsuit.

"You've cut your hair and made a most interesting wardrobe choice."

"Piloting a dart in a dress is rather problematic, but here, away from Father and the gossips, I can wear something more casual."

"Of course. What about your hair?"

"I visited Novam Terram recently. Shorter is all the rage—and I like it."

"Father would not approve…"

She stuck out her tongue.

"…but I do." He hugged her and for a moment pushed away all thoughts of war, intrigue, and death. Then he stepped back and feasted his eyes on the compartment.

Pastel blue bulkheads surrounded him with framed pictures of home, a mural of a party at Camden estate, and a large mirror strategically located. A couch sat before another wall, and curtains hung on a short span of bulkhead near the airlock. Wooden chairs rounded a large carved table at the far end.

"This could be a stateroom on a luxury yacht or liner, and you have a graviton generator—which you could've warned me about. I might have broken my neck in the docking tube."

"I apologize." She laughed. "I forgot Sabre darts don't have gravity—but you figured it out."

"How did you get Father to give you this vessel?"

"He's trying to marry me off to the royal family."

Lucas stepped back. "What? When did this start?"

"Probably at my birth. However, in earnest, two months ago. Both princes showed interest in me at the debutante ball on Novam Terram.

"Draven would show interest in any female. Fat. Homely. Old." He looked hard at his little sister. "Given the right circumstances, any might do."

"I believe my brother has insulted me."

"Forgive me. My intention was to insult Prince Draven, not you."

She laughed. "I know."

"Is there an understanding between you and either of the princes?"

"Oh, by the God of Earth, no. I've maintained a coy aloofness. Thus…" She smiled and spread her arms to display the Curtana-class dart around them. "Not as luxurious as a Sabina, but still rather nice."

"You're playing with fire."

"That's what women of genteel birth do: play with the fire of men. If they do it well, they don't get burned— only rewarded." She cast her brother a wicked grin.

"Did mother teach you that?"

She nodded.

"You're barely a woman."

"And you're barely a man, only a year older than me, but already a warrior. And speaking of men and women, where is the lady you told me of? You're being most impolite to us both."

Lucas bit his lip. "Uh… before I introduce her, there's something I must say."

"Is she from the theater? An Asiatic belly dancer? What, brother? Just tell me."

He sighed and explained how the Argonaut had received a distress call from an Aux base and that it soon became clear the facility had been attacked by the Valac. "The Aux were all dead, but I found Rachel alive among all the carnage and brought her onboard."

He went on to describe how Prince Draven came to be on the Argonaut and met Rachel during a skirmish in the docking bay.

"You've both had a most exciting time."

"Yes, but I need to keep Rachel and Draven apart."

"Well, that's a noble goal, but what do you need me to do?"

"Take Rachel back to Devon with you."

"Why not send her home?"

"I wish that I knew how." He swallowed and again tried to find the right words.

"What worries you, brother?"

"There's danger in meeting Rachel."

Katherine's eyes widened. "How? Why?"

"Rachel speaks fluent English and claims she's from Earth."

Katherine gaped, then she shook her head as if to clear it. "How could she be?"

"I don't know, but I'd like to find out without anyone getting burned at the stake. Will you help me, sister?"

"You are so trusting. Isn't it more likely that she's a lunatic or an agent of Star Chamber?"

"I don't think so."

She stared at him for a moment and then gave a slow nod. "Yes, I'll help you." She turned to the airlock. "I'd love to meet the Daughter of Earth." She approached the hatch.

As he followed, Lucas wondered how his sister, who had been tutored only in the knowledge and skills deemed proper for a woman of high birth, had learned of the Seeker legend.

Chapter 14

Aboard the Lady Katherine
In the Brittany star system

Still confused, Lucas watched Katherine disappeared into the open airlock. With so many things to do, he'd have to ask her how she learned of the old Seeker story some other time.

"Greetings, Rachel. I am Katherine," his sister's voice said from the airlock.

As Katherine continued to speak, Lucas realized he understood less than half the words. His sister spoke English. The best universities commonly taught dead languages, but his little sister never had formal schooling. He wondered what exactly her tutors had taught her all those years.

Katherine beamed a whimsical smile as she stepped back into the main compartment. "You chastised me for wearing a flight suit, but you keep your new belle in military clothes."

"There are no women's clothes on a warship, and she was wearing nothing when I found her."

"Well, that must have been exciting for you." Katherine cast him a wicked grin. "Do you really think she could be the Daughter of—"

"This is dangerous, not an amusement." Lucas scowled.

Her smile faded. "You're right about the danger brother, but let's not dwell on that right now."

Rachel exited the airlock, followed by Konrad.

Katherine stepped close to Lucas. "For now, I'm just glad my big brother is safe and we have this time together. How long may you remain?"

"Mere minutes, I fear."

The chime for an incoming holoview call sounded.

Katherine turned to the controls. Her eyes widened. "Father is calling."

Lucas looked to Rachel and Konrad.

Konrad grasped Rachel's arm.

Lucas motioned for them to retreat into the airlock. Turning to his sister he asked. "Will the holoview center on you?"

"Yes."

"Then you'd better answer it."

Katherine frowned and slowly faced the center of the compartment. "Holoview on." She forced a smile. "Greetings, Father."

A multi-dimensional image of their father appeared in the center of the room.

Lucas saluted his father. "Fleet Admiral Baldwin, it's a surprise to see you."

Konrad steered Rachel back into the airlock.

"Why did you contact us, Father?" Katherine smiled. "I thought you would be busy."

"I *am* busy," Father thundered. "The Orion fleet is about to jump into battle, but then I'm informed my daughter's ship is in the system—even though I told her to keep the vessel close to home."

"Sorry, Father. I wanted to see Lucas."

Their father's eyes locked on Lucas and seemingly, through him. "You don't appear to be injured. Why aren't you on your ship?"

"I'm just taking a moment to visit my sister."

Father nodded his silver-topped head. The faintest hint of a smile appeared.

"According to reports, you've done reasonably well—so far." His gaze returned to its normal sternness. "The Valac have engaged our forces in several systems. Return to your ship and prepare for combat." He turned to Katherine. "Return home now. And change into something befitting my daughter before you arrive."

"Yes, Father."

The image dissolved.

"Always so nice to speak with you, Father." Katherine rolled her eyes. She turned toward the airlock and spoke in English.

Rachel reappeared, followed by Konrad.

Katherine hugged Lucas. "I'll get Rachel to Devon and find a way to hide her. Now you'd better return to your ship before Father calls again." She looked to Rachel and again spoke in English.

"No!" Tears welled in Rachel's eyes and rolled down her cheeks. She clutched Lucas's hand and held tight.

"Sister, what did you say?"

"Ah, only that she would be traveling with me and that you and the helot had to leave."

Lucas glanced at Konrad, who nodded.

Except for his mother and sister, no one had ever cried at his departing. Lucas gently squeezed Rachel's hand. "Sister, translate what I say to Rachel."

Katherine nodded.

Lucas took a deep breath and then spoke. "We're at war with the monsters that tried to kill you. Duty calls me away, but in my absence, my sister Katherine will protect you. If Earth exists then when I return we will find it and take you safely there." He lifted her hand to his lips and gave it a gentle kiss. "I promise. But for now I must say goodbye."

After Katherine finished translating, Rachel wiped away her tears, nodded, and kissed him on the cheek.

Back aboard the military dart, Lucas disengaged from his sister's ship and rushed toward the Argonaut. When they'd ventured several hundred miles apart, the dart's sensors revealed a Mage Tunnel forming near The Lady Katherine. Within seconds, his sister's ship raced across the event horizon and disappeared.

Lucas leaned back into the pilot seat. His home had always been full of people, nobles, officers, servants, and hangers on, but only two people had been friends, Tybalt and Katherine. Now Tybalt served as a senior officer and less as a friend. Katherine would soon be trillions of miles away.

However, thoughts of another lady now flitted through his mind. Beautiful, even in an oversized uniform, and brave enough to fight the Valac. Sadly, she would soon be trillions of miles away also. He hoped both ladies would remain safe.

Lucas sighed and turned to Konrad. "I appreciate your help today."

"I thank you for the kindness and understanding you've shown the Daughter of Earth."

"Our actions may get us both executed."

Konrad nodded. "All of this intrigue will give me gray hair."

Lucas turned toward him and smiled, but he wondered if Konrad had been involved in earlier conspiracy and intrigue. He imagined standing before Star Chamber and then burning at the stake with Konrad on one side and Tybalt on the other. He shuddered.

Minutes later, they docked with the Argonaut. As they exited the shuttle, the jump alarm sounded. Lucas braced for the familiar nausea.

The battle stations alarm blared.

A booming voice announced. "All hands to battle stations. The ship will jump to Prior Four in one minute. The mining facility and naval base are under attack."

Lucas sighed. He would soon be in combat again.

*　*　*

Rachel stared in awe as a whirling vortex bubble of light and shadow opened before them. "What is that?"

Next to her, in the pilot's seat, Katherine's fingers danced over the controls. "We call it a Mage Tunnel. Pull the straps over your shoulder and tighten them around you."

When Rachel complied, Katherine tapped the screen before her, and a roar filled the ship. A weight pushed

Rachel her into the seat as the weird bubble in space grew larger and disappeared into a kaleidoscope of colors she'd seen earlier with Lucas.

The roar faded and the pressure disappeared. Rachel adjusted her position in the chair. It hurt her to leave both Lucas and Konrad, the two men who'd shown her friendship. However, Katherine seemed nice, spoke English, and it would be good to talk with another girl about her age.

She tried to relax and watch Katherine. "What are you doing now?"

"Setting the automatos controls." Katherine's fingers tapped and slid across the screens before her. "Now we can talk without the distraction of piloting." Katherine turned to Rachel with a bemused expression. "We certainly make a fashion statement, with you in a baggy military uniform and me in a pilot's jumpsuit."

Rachel smiled weakly, unsure of her point. "Rather unfeminine, I suppose."

Katherine's accented English sounded similar to Konrad's, forcing Rachel to listen closely.

"Yes." Katherine grinned. "Especially the trousers. My brother, Lucas, mentioned there weren't appropriate clothes for you onboard the Argonaut." She pursed her lips. "Sometimes I chide my brother about his naiveté. I may be younger, but in some ways I'm the more worldly." Her eyes locked on Rachel. "We need to establish a few details before we proceed."

"Okay."

"Who are you?"

"Um… my name is Rachel. Rachel Grace Harper."

"Three names?"

Rachel nodded.

"Does your father have a profession?"

"His occupation?" Rachel, still struggling with accent and word differences, wasn't sure she understood.

Katherine nodded.

"He's an engineer."

He runs engines?

"No." Rachel shook her head. "He's an aerospace engineer."

Katherine's brow furrowed. "Where does he practice this occupation?"

"Seattle, Washington."

Katherine frowned.

"The United States."

Katherine shook her head.

How could such an advanced human society not know of Seattle or even the United States? Rachel suggested, "Earth?"

"Ah, we reach the crux of the issue. How can I know that you really hail from Earth and aren't an agent for Star Chamber?"

The ominous tone of the question sent a chill through Rachel. "I'm not any sort of agent, and I don't know what Star Chamber is, but a man named Tybalt said I should give this to you when you asked for proof."

Katherine's expression softened at the mention of Tybalt. Rachel handed her the dinner bag.

Katherine opened it. "Food?"

Rachel shrugged. "I didn't look inside."

With a wary eye on Rachel, Katherine probed the bag. "A meat pie and several vitabars. Not what I'd wish to eat."

She set the items on a nearby shelf. Then she pulled a clear drink container out and examined it. Chucks of ice floated in a beverage, but one large chunk sat on the bottom. Katherine opened the bottle, reached in, and, spilling some liquid, retrieved the object.

As Rachel watched, the spilt fluid disappeared into the floor.

Katherine held the object close to her eyes. "This is a data crystal."

Rachel had seen similar crystals on the ship and with the monsters on the planet, but she had little idea of their purpose.

Katherine waved the crystal back and forth and then wiped it on her sleeve. She moved to some sort of computer station near the rear of the compartment, and Rachel followed. Katherine she plugged the crystal into a socket on the device.

Tybalt appeared directly in front of Rachel. She gasped and stepped to the side.

The image remained motionless, like a picture hanging on the air.

Rachel turned back to Katherine. "Will it move or talk?"

A smile grew on Katherine's face as she stared at the image. "Yes, I believe so." She stepped toward the computer.

The image of Tybalt glided to face her.

Katherine swiped her hand across a nearby locker, opened it, and removed a pistol-like device. Cool determination etched her face as she locked eyes on Rachel. "My dear friend Tybalt is clearly sending me a message. I will hear it and ascertain the truth of this matter, and depending upon it, you will live or die."

Chapter 15

Aboard the Lady Katherine Traversing a Mage Tunnel

Rachel stared at the weapon pointed at her. "Everything I've said is true."

"I want to believe you, but I will not have my loved ones caught up in a Star Chamber search for traitors or a lunatic's delusion." Katherine tapped the screen to her side.

The holographic image of Tybalt remained stoic and speechless.

A computer voice spoke in the strange language Rachel had recently heard so often.

Katherine bent toward a nearby screen, glanced at Rachel, then continued.

Red laser light scanned her face.

With eyes again fixed on Rachel, she pressed her thumb to the adjacent screen.

Rachel thought she heard the names "Katherine" and "Baldwin," but the computer voice and strange words jumbled together. A beep sounded, followed by more jumbled words.

"Two people are needed to unlock the crystal."
Katherine sat in the pilot's chair. "I suppose you're the
second person."

Rachel stepped forward.

Katherine raised her hand and halted her. "There's a
terminal behind you."

Rachel retreated toward the device but kept her eyes
on the pistol. Rachel longed for people like Lucas and
Konrad who believed her.

"Proceed," Katherine commanded.

If Rachel couldn't verify her story, Katherine would
kill her and dump her body in space. She'd only met
Tybalt briefly, but he seemed to want to help. Perhaps
the contents of the crystal would verify her story. Worry
burned in her stomach like an ulcer as she turned to the
workstation beside her.

Following Katherine's example, Rachel leaned down
and placed her face directly in front. Red light shined
into her eye. When it stopped, she pressed her thumb to
a blank space on the screen.

The computer voice said, "Specimen," followed by
what sounded like numbers and then unintelligible words.

"Specimen? What did it say?"

Katherine stared at the image of Tybalt, still standing
in the center of the compartment. "The computare said,
'Specimen 7562 identified. Automatos erase countdown
terminated.'"

"What does that mean?"

"For some reason the computare thinks you are a
specimen." Katherine smiled at Rachel. "The device

required eye and thumb scans from both of us to release the information. Since we provided what it needed, it will not erase itself."

"Scan? My eye? I don't remember being scanned. How did someone get an image of my eye or a fingerprint?"

"I can't answer those questions. Perhaps they scanned you while on that planet with the Aux, or when brought onboard the Argonaut." She shook her head. "Though the sailors and marines wouldn't refer to you as a specimen. They would have asked your name. Hopefully, we'll find answers."

Katherine tapped the display beside her and the image of Tybalt flickered.

"Dearest Katherine …"

Rachel understood the first two words, but after that she comprehended little. However, as the message continued, Katherine's expression softened and the gun drooped to her side.

After nearly a minute, Tybalt stopped speaking.

With her gaze still fixed upon the image, Katherine smiled.

Rachel relaxed some, now that her host appeared less threatening.

Katherine tapped the display and once again Tybalt spoke, but this time in English.

"Now that you fully understand what I'm asking you to do, it would be wise if both you, and Rachel, see the following images. However, I must warn you some are very troubling." Tybalt paused. "Tap the controller when both of you are ready to continue."

Without so much as a glance at Rachel, Katherine smacked the screen.

Tybalt dissolved in a swirl of light. Then a blue and green world appeared in the center of the compartment.

Rachel instantly recognized the continents of North and South America. "That's Earth!"

Katherine stepped closer to Rachel with the gun still at her side. "I've seen a few maps, but I don't recognize this."

"It is." Rachel pointed. "That's Hawaii just coming into view. There's Japan and China. India is coming up and—"

"The Holy Lands, Africa, and Europe—this part of the planet I've seen on old maps." Astonished, she stepped closer and put her hand over England, and then over the Middle East. She whispered, "All my life I've dreamed that it still existed. Could it be real?"

"This looks like a picture of Earth from space. It seems real to me, but I've never been in space... well, before this."

They continued to watch as the planet rotated.

Rachel pointed. "I'm from there, a city called Seattle."

Katherine tilted her head to the side, and her eyes narrowed, but she said nothing.

After several more rotations of the planet image, it faded into nothing.

"I wouldn't call that image troubling." Katherine grinned.

"To me it's like I was there just a few days ago, but Konrad told me that according to your history Earth, was destroyed centuries ago."

"Konrad?"

"The Seeker who came with me and Lucas."

Katherine nodded. "Yes. The helot would have shared an interesting version of our history."

"So, my world, my family, and everyone I love are dead?"

"You're alive, so I pray they are also." Katherine walked back toward the crystal. "I would think there is more."

Before she reached the crystal, the holographic image of a naked girl appeared. She floated in the air with her arms and legs spread wide.

Katherine looked at the girl's face and gasped.

Rachel could only see the girl's back.

Slowly the image rotated until her front side came into view.

Rachel gazed into her own face. From head to toe, the body remained motionless, but the frightened eyes darted in every direction. Suddenly, the skin dissolved, revealing the muscles below.

Rachel stifled a scream and stumbled back against the wall.

Katherine stopped the display and turned off the projector. "I apologize for this most unsettling image." She shook her head as if struggling to understand. "Tybalt is a... a true friend. He wanted us to see this, so there must be a good reason." For a moment, Katherine said nothing. "I'll continue when—*if* you are ready."

"I don't understand." Rachel gestured toward the center of the compartment.

"I believe the vid is computare-created—not really you."

She recalled the image of her frightened eyes and motionless body with a shudder. "It looked real... so very real." Her head slumped.

Katherine set the gun down, walked to Rachel's side, and touched her shoulder. "Tybalt said these are copies of the Aux data crystals from the planet where you were found. I want to believe that you're from Earth, but I need to see and understand what Tybalt has discovered."

Still staring at the floor, Rachel sighed deeply. "Go ahead." When the image resumed she slowly raised her head.

"That's Aux writing." Katherine pointed to golden swirls that appeared alongside.

"What does it say?" Rachel asked.

"I can read a few words but not any of these."

Next a holographic video of Rachel on a crystal slab appeared. Four centipede-like creatures surrounded her. Two silver streams flowed along her forehead, across her eyelids, and then solidified. Slowly they pulled her eyes open. Additional tendrils held her head motionless and her mouth wide. Lights of various colors danced over her body.

"Those monsters—they're Aux?" She shuddered.

Katherine nodded. "Auxilum, an ally in the war against the Valac."

"One of the few things I remember is lying on a cold table, unable to move—I couldn't even close my eyes— while centipede-like monsters cut, probed, prodded, and stabbed me." The memory remained vivid, but no scars endured to provide evidence.

Katherine's eyes registered shock at these words. "Did you tell Lucas about this?"

"He doesn't speak English. I never had the chance."

Again the image dissolved into nothingness and another holographic display of Rachel, naked and with her arms and legs spread wide appeared.

"Really, again?" Rachel shook her head. *I'm so glad Lucas and Konrad aren't here.* The Earth and Moon appeared beside the image of her. All three rotated in unison.

"Is that the Moon?" Katherine asked.

Rachel nodded "And the Earth."

Golden calligraphy appeared beside all three images.

"What does that say?" Rachel waved an arm at the image.

Katherine stared at the rotating projection. "Something 7562. I think we've determined that's you." She pointed to the planet. "That's the Aux word for Earth—just as you identified it. I don't know that last word, but you said it's the Moon."

The golden twists and whirls of Aux writing appeared beside the Earth. The image centered over the Pacific Northwest region of the United States and then zoomed in like a meteor falling toward the ground. It stopped a few feet above a blonde-haired girl in a dark blue, strapless, floor-length prom dress.

The girl looked into the air, and her eyes filled with terror.

Rachel recognized both the dress and the girl. She gasped as the memories flooded back.

The image dissolved.

"Ryan Brentwood, the football quarterback, was my date to the prom."

Katherine looked confused. "Do you mean promenade?"

"I don't know. I've only heard it called a prom, it's a big dance. My, uh, escort was the leader of the sports team. We had a great time at the dance, but when we left, Ryan took me to his house. I thought his parents would be there, but they weren't, and Ryan... well, he had plans for the night."

Rachel paused and wiped the tears from her eyes. "He wouldn't take me home, so I ran from the house and across a nearby park. That's the last moment I remember on Earth."

Tears flowed freely down her cheeks.

Katherine looked at Rachel as if for the first time. "I believe you and what Tybalt has shown us."

She stepped closer but stopped about twelve feet away.

"Daughter of Earth, I apologize for my rude and threatening behavior. Let us start anew. I am Lady Katherine Charlotte Elizabeth Baldwin, daughter of the Marques of Devon. Both Tybalt and my brother, Lucas, asked me to keep you safe and hidden until they return. I will do so." She curtsied.

"Uh... yes, well, nice to meet you... again." She attempted a similar curtsy but stumbled.

Katherine grinned. "We have much to work on if you are to remain hidden among the people of Terra."

Chapter 16

Onboard the Lady Katherine Traversing a Mage Tunnel

Rachel followed her host into what she called the vestibule.

Katherine glanced over her shoulder and gestured with both arms. "I hardly know where to begin. I have so many questions. You too must have many questions, but first, are you hungry? Let's have dinner, shall we? And then allow me to show you my ship."

As they passed through the compartment, Rachel noticed the airlock where she'd come on board only an hour earlier. While she'd seen that section of the ship before, she hadn't noticed the paintings, mural, mirror, and curtains that made it look elegant, not at all like a spaceship.

Rachel walked to the round wooden table. "Is this where you eat?"

"Rarely. This is more of a meeting room. The dining room is farther aft."

"Aft?"

"Toward the rear of the ship." Katherine continued down a narrow passageway that reminded Rachel of a train corridor.

"Should we have left the bridge empty like that?" Rachel glanced back at the still open hatch.

"It should be fine for now."

"Should… for now?" Rachel mumbled. "Are we the only ones on the ship?"

"Yes. Isn't it fantastic?" Katherine stopped, opened a side door, and entered.

Rachel followed.

"This is the dining room, or as my brother would say, the mess deck." Katherine shook her head. "Men."

A long wooden table stood in the center, surrounded by ten chairs. Carved legs and etched designs decorated the wood. Huge paintings and curtains hung from the walls. They continued on through another door to a room that vaguely reminded her of a kitchen.

Katherine stopped in front of a large display built into the wall. Images of food appeared in varying combinations.

"This can only do such simple things." She pressed a picture of what looked like casserole. "When I get home, I'll have the cook make us some real food. You must tell me about Earth cuisine."

Ding.

Two plates heaped high with food slid out of what vaguely looked like a microwave, but no food had been put into it.

Katherine continued to talk as they walk to the table with their plates.

As they ate, memories of an earlier dinner returned to Rachel. Christmas songs played softly as a gentle snow fell outside. Rachel recalled a decorated tree encom-passed by presents as she had hurried through the living room toward smells of turkey, stuffing, and cranberries. She entered the room and turned to her mother as the memory faded.

Tears welled in Rachel's eyes. Her head slumped.

Katherine touched her arm. "What's wrong?"

"When I awoke a few days ago, I didn't even remem-ber my name. Slowly, bits and pieces are coming back." Tears blurred her vision as she looked up at Katherine. "I just remembered a family dinner." She sighed. "I'm never going to see any of them again. They're dead, aren't they?"

Katherine stood and gently hugged her. "All I know is that I'll work to find Earth and your family."

After dinner, she led Rachel to another room. "I designed this to be Lucas's stateroom, but until we reach Devon, it shall be yours." Katherine opened the door and spread her arms wide. "Do you like it?"

Rachel grinned. Her host's enthusiasm reminded her of friends showing off their first cars. She stepped into a room twice the size of her parents' bedroom back in Seattle. Huge rugs covered what looked like a wood floor. Several paintings of country scenes hung on tan walls. Gold curtains hung on either side of a huge bed. A large wooden dresser stood nearby.

"Like it? Yes… uh, yes, this is nice. Very nice." *How rich do you have to be to own your own cruise ship?*

Rachel opened a door to what looked like a small empty room with just a mirror on one wall and three other doors. She pointed. "Where do these go?"

"One leads to a closet, that one is to the bathroom, and the last is for the privy chamber."

Rachel wore all the clothes she possessed and had no need of a closet or dresser, and she had no idea what a privy chamber might be. However, she was grateful to know the location of a bathroom.

"Come. I'll show you the rest of the ship." Katherine hurried out of the room and down the narrow passageway to the next door. "This is my room."

The design resembled the previous chamber, but with more pastel colors. Clothes lay scattered over an unmade bed and on the rug beside it.

Perhaps noticing Rachel's gaze, Katherine giggled. "I should have brought my ladies maid." She looked Rachel up and down. "Would you like a pilot's suit like mine or perhaps a dress?"

"A jumpsuit would be fine."

Katherine nodded. "When we seeing the ship, I'll get you clothes and some other things you might need."

Katherine continued aft.

"What's in that room?" Rachel asked.

"Oh, that's the cargo bay." Katherine pulled open a heavy steel hatch. "Boring and mostly empty."

Rachel glanced inside. It spread larger than she would've thought, about half the size of her high school gym back home. A dozen crates sat stacked near the rear of the otherwise empty space.

Katherine continued on, leaving the door open.

Rachel followed. "What's that big red button? I noticed one on the bridge and in the vestibule.

"They're beside each airtight hatch." She tapped on a doorframe. "In an emergency, the automatos system closes this door, one in the vestibule, and one behind the bridge. You can stop the door by pressing this button." Katherine continued on to the engine room which she described as "boring."

Rachel estimated that the tour, minus dinner, took about an hour. When they left the engine room, she shook her head. "How do you run this entire ship by yourself?"

"The original configuration does call for a crew of five, but if I had hired them, Father would've been informed and said no. He wanted me to keep the ship in the Devon system."

"Can you pilot this alone?"

"Sure, on short trips and with the advanced automatos controls I had installed. We should be fine."

Rachel pursed her lips but said nothing as they walked back to her new bedroom.

"I do need to check everything on the bridge before retiring for the evening. I'll knock in the morning for breakfast." Katherine hurried along the passageway.

Rachel called "good night" to Katherine and entered the expansive room. Now alone, she dashed straight to the bathroom.

As the light came on, she discovered the name described the function—a room where you took a bath. A round tiled tub, nearly three feet deep and six feet across, filled most of the small space. Tiles on the floor created a mosaic. She did need a bath, and the tub was inviting, but right then she needed something else even more.

She hurried to the privy chamber. At the rear of the tiny room sat an etched golden bowl. It appeared too elegant for the purpose, but closer inspection confirmed what she'd hoped. She used it and sighed. A button on the wall flushed it much like the airline version or those on Lucas's military ship.

Back in the bathroom, she fiddled with the controls, scalding and freezing herself until she got the temperature right. Then she filled the tub and floated in the middle. As tension flowed from her, memories returned and her tears joined with the water of the tub.

*   *   *

After a fitful night, Rachel lay in bed wondering if she'd ever see Earth or her family again. A loud grumbling from her stomach made her wish for a breakfast with her parents of eggs and bacon. She wondered what time Katherine planned to eat. They hadn't discussed much along those lines the night before.

She didn't want to dress in the military clothes, but those were all she had. Katherine hadn't brought the promised items. For several minutes she wondered what to do.

"Lady Katherine requests to enter," a female computer voice announced.

Rachel jumped from bed and pulled the blanket around her. "Oh, sure. Uh, come in."

The door swung open and Katherine bounded in. "I brought you clean clothes and other things. When you're ready, meet me in the dining room. I'll have breakfast ready."

After the meal of what looked like eggs and sausages but didn't taste like it, Rachel sat beside Katherine on the bridge as she tapped on various points of the screen for nearly a minute and waved her arm near the display. "Why do you do that with your arm?" Rachel mimicked the motion.

Katherine grinned. "It's not my arm that I'm waving. It's the bracelet on my wrist. It's like... like a key."

Rachel had noticed it before—a half-inch wide band of shiny gold. A design of intertwined branches and leaves covered most of it, but one area remained smooth polished metal. A shiny coat covered all of it. "I just thought it was jewelry."

"It is also that, and a key, and much more."

"Do only women have them? I didn't see one on Lucas or Konrad."

"Almost everyone does. Lucas has a plain one, but when serving in the military, men don't wear them. If they were captured or killed, the bracelets would provide too much information and access to the Valac. Who's Konrad?"

"The older man with me when I arrived."

Katherine thought for a moment. "The helot? No, they usually don't have bracelets." She turned back to the controls.

Rachel stared at the swirling colors of the Mage Tunnel on the view screen pondering all this new information. Certainly the Earth existed on the day the Aux kidnapped her, but did it now? How long had she been asleep or unconscious?

Looking at the spaceship around her, perhaps 300 years had indeed passed. Sadness weighed on her. If Earth no longer remained, she would need to accept that everyone she'd known died long ago, and she'd spend her life in this strange new world.

A blue light blinked on the panel before her. "What does that mean?"

Katherine pursed her lips and tapped on the display near the light. "I think it's a sign that we'll be dropping into normal space soon."

"Uh… *think?*"

"I'm still learning, but that's what the automatos pilot appears to indicate."

Rachel fidgeted in her seat. They were traveling through deep space, and Katherine apparently had only a learner's permit.

Katherine tapped on the display. "Sarah, are we about to return to normal space?"

The female voice Rachel had heard in her bedroom now filled this compartment. "Detectors indicate a return to normal space in less than ten minutes."

Katherine dropped the ship to normal space, and minutes later they shot into another Mage Tunnel. For the remainder of that day and much of the next, Katherine drilled Rachel on the basics of Terran speech and etiquette, but it all seemed so different, old-fashioned in many ways, and filled with new words, strange customs, and bizarre aliens.

"I wish we had more time," Rachel lamented. "When we enter normal space, will we be at your home planet?"

"Are you nervous about our arrival?" Katherine didn't wait for a reply. "I guess I am also. We still have two jumps to make. I need to drop into Efford, make a course correction, and then jump a little more than a Geller to the Devon system." She made adjustments on the display in front of her and waved the bracelet."

"What's a Geller?"

Katherine turned from the display. "It's a measurement. The distance light travels in a year."

"On Earth it's called a light-year."

"I wouldn't have thought Earth knew about such things before its destruction." Katherine shrugged. "We'll both have to change into proper clothing before we arrive at Devon. Until then, you need more practice. Curtsy one more time for me. You must get this right, or people will notice."

Rachel sighed again. She felt silly curtsying in a jumpsuit, but she didn't want to dress in what Terran society considered proper women's clothing. Complete with a corset, the attire appeared little different than that of Earth's Victorian era. Rachel stood, pasted a smile on her face, placed one foot behind the other, bent her knees, and bowed her head.

Katherine smiled. "A possible curtsy. Now about those greetings—"

As Katherine continued her instruction the jump alarm sounded. A couple of minutes later the kaleidoscope of colors on the main pilot screen dissolved into black, speckled with tiny dots. One orb of yellow light stood out clearly.

"Is that Efford?" Rachel pointed to the speck of light.

Before Katherine could answer, the image of a man in uniform appeared on several screens and at the center of the compartment. Alarms sounded behind him, and dust floated around him. "Warning to all civilian ships: the Efford system is under attack by the Valac. Jump immediately."

Katherine tapped the screen and the image disappeared. She leaned close to the console. Her fingers flew over the controls.

The calm computer voice of Sarah sounded all around them. "Two Valac ships are approaching on the starboard side at high velocity."

Chapter 17

Onboard the Argonaut
Near the Prior star system

In full combat gear and with a lance slung over one shoulder, Lucas stood in the Marine Operations Center. He stared at the holoview image of twenty Valac warships on the hunt in the Prior system. Most of the enemy vessels circled the fourth planet.

He frowned. If this attack followed the pattern of earlier engagements, no human life remained at the mining facility on the surface.

All eyes turned to Tybalt as he entered the compartment.

Knowing that Tybalt had just been briefed by the command staff, anxiety churned inside of Lucas. "It's clear this is no raid. They intend to hold the system, don't they?"

Tybalt nodded. "Before the Valac destroyed it, the navy satellite probe revealed warriors on the surface of Prior Four. They've attacked the mining facilities in both the Bodmin system and here. They want to cripple us in this sector. It's possible this is a diversion to draw the bulk of our navy here and attack elsewhere."

Lucas pondered the idea. "What does naval command think?"

"They don't tell me such things." Tybalt shrugged. "However, they're not sending more ships or marines. The Pegasus Fleet will attack Bodmin and the Orion will assault Prior."

"They believe this is a feint." Lucas sighed.

Together they stared at the holo image in silence.

"At least Katherine and Rachel are safe." Tybalt faced Lucas. "Are all your men ready? Are *you* ready?"

Lucas's mouth felt dry. He nodded.

Tybalt squeezed his shoulder. "I have some good news."

Lucas cast him a skeptical look. "Other than a Valac withdraw from the system, what good could there be at this moment?"

"You've been promoted to cornet."

"What?" Lucas shook his head. He felt his face flush. He wanted to turn it down. "I'm only seventeen."

"And about to go into battle for the third time." Tybalt grinned. "The generals couldn't keep allowing a cadet to lead marines in combat, so they gave you a regular commission, albeit the lowest one."

Lucas stared at him.

"You have all the skills and courage needed. We'll have the ceremony when we return to Devon." He smiled and patted his friend on the back. "Go inspect your men for combat, Cornet Lucas, and remember, we are the point of the sword."

Lucas took a deep breath. "Victory our only reward."

The jump alarm sounded. Lucas saluted his friend and senior officer and then turned to join his men. Within minutes he would be in battle.

* * *

Onboard the Lady Katherine
Near the Efford star system

An invisible weight pressed Rachel into her seat.

"By the God of Earth, I'm never leaving Devon again," Katherine shouted as her fingers raced over the controls.

Engines roared. Alarms sounded.

"Valac ships approaching at high velocity on both the port and starboard," Sarah's calm voice reported.

Katherine looked up. "Silence all alarms!"

The compartment fell quiet.

Rachel pointed to a bubble of swirling color off the bow. "Is that our Mage Tunnel? Can we jump?"

"It's still forming." Katherine pressed on the display before her. "I'm lining the ship up for entry."

"Collision warning," Sarah announced. "Valac wasps will impact in five seconds."

Katherine thrust her hand along the screen.

The acceleration pressed Rachel into her seat, they entered the bubble, and that weird feeling returned to her stomach.

"We've jumped." Katherine exhaled. "We'll be in the tunnel for about an hour, and then we'll exit at the edge of the Devon system."

Nothing about this felt like a trip home. Rachel tensed, waiting for the next monster to jump out and attack her. That ominous feeling rarely faded. Her eyes swept the compartment, searching for any threat. "The Valac didn't follow us into the tunnel?"

"No." Katherine grinned. "The entrance collapses moments after we cross."

"They were so close."

Katherine frowned. "Detectors don't work well in a Mage Tunnel, but I'll do a search."

Rachel unstrapped from her seat and stood. She walked along the edge of the compartment, glancing at screens and thinking. Devon might not be home, but she'd been among weird creatures and spaceships for... she didn't know how long. It would be good to spend time on a more familiar world of humans.

Rachel heard a gasp. She spun around. "What?"

Katherine stared at the display. "A Valac warship and two wasps are behind us in the tunnel."

Rachel hurried and stood behind Katherine in the pilot's seat. She dug her fingers into the material as she leaned close. "Can we stay ahead of them?"

"No."

"Can't we go faster?"

"It doesn't work like that." Katherine shook her head. "You can slow down, but not go faster. The tunnel absorbs energy, so you slowly lose momentum and eventually return to normal space. The Valac were going faster when they entered, so they're closing the distance between us. The warship is already in firing range, but they may not want to destabilize the tunnel."

She glanced at the screen.

"The wasps will catch up to us in less than thirty minutes. They'll probably try to board us then."

"Then we'll fight them."

Katherine's eyes widened and fear etched her face. "I can't... can't set the automatos controls and fight Valac."

"Then I will." Rachel grabbed the pistol from the nearby locker. "I've used one like this before, but how do you turn it on?"

"Lucas told me you've fought." Hope and confusion mingled in Katherine's face as she placed her thumb on a switch. "Push it forward like this. See the red light? It's ready to fire."

She opened a locker, yanked out a rifle-like lance, and did the same. She handed both to Rachel and for several minutes instructed her on aiming and reloading.

"All children here learn to fire a lance in school, but you never did?"

"I did some target shooting with my father and brother, but no. On Earth, weapons training isn't common in school."

"How would you defend yourself against an enemy?"

"It never really came up."

"Among the Kingdoms of Terra the topic is routine." Katherine tapped a nearby screen and a holographic image of the ship appeared. "The Valac try to attach their troop transport wasps to the first smooth area of hull they reach. So they'll probably enter here, just forward from the main engines."

Thud. Thud.

"Two wasps have attached to the hull," Sarah said with an almost cheerful tone.

"Are you ready?"

Near panic, Rachel shoved the pistol into her pocket and nodded.

"Hull breach, main cargo bay," Sarah advised.

"The Valac will soon enter this ship. We need only minutes to reach home. I pray you can hold them off." Katherine turned back to the controls. "I'll join you as soon as I've set the controls for our arrival at the Devon system."

Unable to speak, Rachel nodded and then ran aft. She rushed through the vestibule and along the narrow passageway past the galley and their bedrooms, or berths as Katherine had called them.

In seconds she reached the cargo bay. The heavy steel hatch remained open. Rachel stepped into the largest open space on the ship. At the far end, two round holes had burned through the ceiling, but she saw no Valac. Only the crates, lashed to the deck just forward from the holes, blocked her view.

Where were the Valac? Were they waiting, perhaps behind the boxes? She swallowed and stepped closer.

She heard only the rattle from an air duct.

Rachel took another step. Sweat trickled down her face.

Clicking sounded from above.

She stopped. Her eyes darted from hole to hole and then to the crates. She slid a foot forward.

Valac scurried from behind the crates and through the holes above.

Rachel screamed and fired at the nearest.

The monster in front dropped, but the others formed a semi-circle around her.

She stepped back and fired again. There weren't that many. If she kept backing up and shooting she might be able to hold them off. Another blast brought a third Valac to the floor.

Their tails rose in near unison. She'd seen them fire stingers both on the planet and aboard the Argonaut, but they had never shot at her.

She took another step back and fired again.

Hearing a noise behind, she glanced over her shoulder. A Valac stood directly behind her blocking the hatch. *How did it get there?*

Then she noticed one hanging above. They'd skittered over her head, out of sight, and now five of them surrounded her. She could kill one, maybe two, but they would tear her to pieces before she killed them all.

The Valac tightened the circle around her and stopped. Then in unison the monsters began their strange melody. Some notes ranged so low that they vibrated through Rachel. Other notes ran up the scale until they hurt her ears and then faded into silence.

A thought formed in her mind. They wouldn't hurt her. They never intended to hurt her.

The jump alarm sounded, and moments later the weird feeling washed through her. They were in normal space at the edge of the Devon system.

The clamber of footfalls resounded in the passageway. Katherine came into view with a scream.

The nearest Valac snapped his mandible in her direction.

Katherine lowered her weapon to fire.

"No! Stop!" Rachel thrust her arms out.

The Valac held their positions.

Katherine stuttered as her eyes narrowed. Confusion spread across her face.

Rachel turned from one Valac to another as they resumed their song. Strange images of death and despair welled within her. Their dark black color seemed to fade. They didn't want to fight.

Hesitantly, she turned to the nearest Valac. "I think I understand what you're telling me, but you've got to leave, or you'll die."

Chapter 18

Onboard the Argonaut
Near the Prior star system

Cornet Lucas dared not speak. His dry mouth and queasy stomach threatened to embarrass him. Mustering what he hoped appeared as a stern demeanor, he stepped into the berthing compartment.

Sergeant Collins called the men to attention.

With the sergeant beside him, Lucas walked to the first man and inspected his lance and combat gear. With a nod he stepped to the next.

When he completed the inspection, he and Sergeant Collins finished readying their own gear in the nearby storage area.

Lucas recalled countless combat preparation drills at the academy. The lance charge was green. Set to kill. Fifty rounds loaded.

Just four months earlier he'd been a student, eager to depart on his first training mission. Those days now seemed long ago. He looked down at the additional ammunition on the bandolier, then he slid his knife into its sheath.

Finally, he and Sergeant Collins stood close and checked each other's gear.

The sergeant locked eyes with Lucas. "I watched you on Lepeus Delta and during the fight in the cargo bay. You'll do fine, sir."

Lucas drank water from a nearby bottle. "Thank you, Sergeant."

He grabbed his helmet and lance and headed back to the men. Reaching the compartment again, he paused. Should he say something inspirational or uplifting?

"All marines to the launch bay." The baritone voice of the officer of the deck boomed over the ship vox system. "Battle deployment in fifteen minutes."

Lucas lifted his lance high. "We are the point of the sword!"

"Victory our only reward!" his men chanted in return.

Lucas led them past the operations center and down the passageway to the launch bay. He stood at the foot of the ramp as they trotted past him and into the dart. Only then did Lucas walk up the ramp with a confident stride. It was an act but one he felt needed to be done.

"Uniforms on full automatos." He watched as one by one the men blended in with the hull of the dart and disappeared, except for their uncovered heads. "Helmets on and locked. Sound off through your ethercomm."

After Lucas locked his helmet on and strapped himself in, Tybalt's voice came over the secure link. "We're approaching on the dark side of the planet. We'll launch all darts while still on the night side, but you'll land on the daylight side of the terminator just after local dawn. Link up with me as soon as possible. Understood?"

"Yes," Lucas squeaked. Despite drinking water, his throat felt dry.

Tybalt chuckled. "I'm glad no one asked me anything the first time I launched into combat. I just sat there beside Victor shaking and praying all the way to the surface."

"You were just a squire," Lucas replied. "Not the cornet in charge of a platoon."

"True, but you won't be alone when you reach the planet. Remember, as soon as you land, link the unit and your ethercomm with me."

Lucas pulled the last strap tight across his chest. "I will."

The lights in the dart faded. The baritone voice came again over the ship comm, "Deployment in five, four, three, two, launch!"

* * *

Onboard the Lady Katherine
At the edge of the Devon star system

The Valac stood aside as Rachel sprinted into the passageway.

Katherine stepped backward and pointed her lance at Rachel. "Why didn't they hurt you? How could you talk to them?"

Staring at the lance, Rachel stopped. "I don't know. We communicated somehow, but I don't know how or why."

"They didn't kill us." Katherine looked past Rachel. "They're just leaving."

Rachel looked over her shoulder. The Valac departed, dragging the four she'd killed with them. In seconds the cargo bay stood empty. She felt a soft breeze swirl around her from two directions. Her ears popped.

"Warning. Hull breech at frames 451 and 452 of the cargo bay," Sarah's calm computer voice reported. "Shutting all airtight hatches."

The door to engineering slid shut

The wind blew through her hair in toward the cargo bay.

Katherine gasped. "We need to get to the bridge before the hatches shut." She turned and ran.

Rachel started to follow but stopped. Seeing the cargo bay door wide open, she grabbed hold. The heavy metal door hung on simple hinges. If they shut the hatch, the air loss would stop. She called to Katherine, but the wind swallowed her voice. Using both hands, Rachel pulled with all her strength.

The wind caught the hatch, ripped it from her hands, and slammed it. The latch bent into the door frame. A gap of less than an inch remained between the hatch and frame. Rachel tried to move the latch and shut the door, but couldn't budge it against the growing gale.

She turned and ran with her head down. Grasping at every knob, lever, and pipe, she pulled herself against the storm. Each door or pipe she clutched tingled of cold. Her hand slipped as she grabbed a damp pipe. As if climbing a steep slope, she dragged herself forward, and struggled for breath. Had Katherine abandoned her? Would this be where she'd die?

No. She'd endured too much to die here.

Rachel pushed forward. Tears from the cold wind clouded her eyes. Gripping a pipe with one hand, she wiped her face with the other. Ahead, she spotted the vestibule emergency hatch three-quarters of the way down but not moving.

Leaning hard into the wind, she struggled forward and with one great push lunged under the door, into the vestibule behind the bridge.

Katherine lifted her hand from the large red button, and the door dropped with a clang.

"Air-tight hatches sealed," Sarah announced. "All compartments aft of frame 85 have lost atmosphere."

Rachel lay on the floor gasping for air. When Rachel's breathing returned to normal, Katherine helped her stand, and they returned to the seats on the bridge. After a moment, Rachel turned to Katherine.

"Thank you." Rachel's gaze dropped. "When you pointed the lance at me, I was worried that you might think I was some sort of spy. When you ran, I thought you might leave me to die in the passageway, but you saved my life."

"I did wonder what you were." Katherine ran a hand through her hair. "The Valac have never used humans as infiltrators or spies, and I did see the four bodies in the cargo bay. I don't know how you did it, but I'm grateful the other Valac left."

Rachel shook her head. She didn't understand the images of despair that lingered in her mind. She only had a feeling that the Valac weren't the real enemy. Still, uncertainty lingered. "I have no idea how that happened."

"Indeed, you are an enigma."

For several minutes they talked while Katherine made final adjustments for entry into the Devon system.

"Devon is a beautiful green planet. Much like the old texts describe Earth. I believe you will like it." She made one more adjustment and leaned back in her chair with a sigh. "I believe I've had more excitement these last few days than in all the rest of my—"

She leaned forward. Her eyes widened. In a flurry, her fingers moved over the controls.

"Somehow I thought… hoped, they'd be gone, but the Valac warship is only a few hundred yards off our stern."

Rachel leaned close. "From what you've told me, they can't leave the Mage Tunnel without endangering all of us."

"That's correct." Katherine nodded. "Still, this seems like a childhood nightmare. The Valac are right behind us, and we can't get away."

"If the Valac meant to harm us, they would've done so in the cargo bay."

Again Katherine nodded. "I hope they jump away when we arrive at Devon."

The two sat in tense silence as minutes slipped by. When the jump alarm sounded, Rachel grabbed the arms of her seat as Katherine maneuvered the ship back to normal space.

Katherine carefully fingered the controls and then slapped her hand on a large blue digital button. "Devon traffic control, this is the Lady Katherine Baldwin. We have been attacked by Valac and our ship is damaged." Her words were hurried. "We're on standard approach but request immediate jump to the space lift."

Leaning toward the display screen before her, Rachel watched as the Valac warship jumped away.

Occupied with piloting the ship, Katherine didn't notice and began her message again with more urgency.

Before she completed it a second time, a composed male voice filled the bridge. "Lady Katherine, this is Devon Control. We are uploading coordinates now. Upon arrival, proceed to Baldwin docking port two. Immediate jump has been approved."

"The Valac are gone." Rachel pointed to the screen.

Katherine sighed, tapped the jump control, and leaned back in her seat. Minutes later, she shutdown the main engines and used the automatos system as she approached a large space station.

To Rachel it appeared the station had several sets of cables hanging down to the planet below. Boxes rode the cables up and down.

"Is that like an elevator?" She pointed, as her voice rose. "Up to space?"

"What is an elevator?"

"It lifts people and things."

"Then yes, it is. We call it a skylift."

When the station seemed close enough for Rachel to touch, docking clamps clanged.

Katherine shut down the maneuvering engines and turned to Rachel. "I don't know what happened between you and the Valac in the cargo bay. When we have time, we'll need to discuss it, but until we do, say only that you fought the Valac in the compartment and they retreated."

Rachel nodded.

Katherine looked at the environmental controls. "Well, since the cargo bay door never closed, our berths have no atmosphere. So we both shall wear men's clothing when we exit the ship."

"I don't care." Rachel laughed. "On Earth, women wear pants and serve in the military."

"No weapons training in school, but women in the military and wearing trousers? What strange customs." Katherine stepped to the bridge hatch. "Normally, I wouldn't care much about being seen in such clothes. I like how I look in this pilot uniform, but today it is a worry."

"You're home and safe." Rachel eyed her. "Why would you worry about your clothes?"

"Remember, Daughter of Earth." Katherine frowned. "My brother asked me to hide you from those who would kill you."

Wishing she hadn't asked, Rachel nodded.

"I worry that as the daughter of a marcher lord, missing during a major Valac offensive, my disappearance may have attracted attention." She stepped toward the foyer and the airlock. "That and our clothes will ensure that within minutes of our stepping from this ship, we will be on all of the vids. You have shown courage before the Valac, but are you ready to face Terran society?"

Chapter 19

Onboard a marine dart
Over Prior Four

The dart sped toward the surface like a meteor falling from the sky. The pilot had control, but Lucas felt faint, and vomit surged in this throat. His suit pressed tight around his torso, attempting to keep him conscious. Falling through the sky at incredible speed helped avoid Valac defensive fire, but it unnerved him.

A thunderous boom echoed through the dart, and it shuddered and swayed.

Lucas slammed into the seat harness. The dart had been hit.

Metal scraped and tore.

A gaping hole opened in the hull across from Lucas.

Harnesses broke.

Men screamed as they were ripped from their seats and thrown through the growing breach into the darkness.

The dart spun wildly.

The harness dug into his shoulders and chest. Images of Rachel, Katherine, and Tybalt raced through his mind.

A calm clarity took ahold of him. In seconds the dart would crash into the ground, and he would die.

*   *   *

Onboard the Devon Skylift
Over Devon Prime

"No." Rachel's eyes went wide. "Of course I'm not ready to face these people."

Katherine opened the airlock door. "It may be a long time before we find Earth—if we ever do. We can't hide in here until then, so I suggest we get moving. I'm sure the crowd is already forming."

Rachel's heart pounded. As they entered the skylift, she looked about. They'd entered a large, circular room that resembled an airline boarding lounge. Huge windows gave a spectacular view of stars, a moon, and part of a green and blue planet. A waist-high partition separated her and Katherine from eight female onlookers.

"From what you described, I expected more people to be here."

Katherine looked about and frowned. "So did I."

As Rachel watched, the long gowns of all the women slowly changed hue. She turned to ask Katherine about the color changes, but she hadn't stopped.

The spectators ignored Rachel and followed Katherine, and several held up their arms revealing silver bracelets. She wondered if the device also took pictures. One more question to ask Katherine when she caught up.

As she came alongside, Rachel spotted a girl about their age hurrying toward them. She wore a simple black dress with a full skirt that hung down to her ankles, similar to that of the ladies who gawked nearby but much plainer. Her long blonde hair had been pulled tight into a bun.

The young woman curtsied. "Welcome home, Lady Katherine."

Rachel noticed a plain copper band on her right wrist.

"Naomi, I'm surprised to see you here, but glad." Katherine stopped and smiled. "My ship is damaged and unable to land on the planet. Rachel and I will need appropriate clothing and air transport to Camden."

"Camden, My Lady? This time of year?"

"Yes," Katherine said flatly. "Oh and this is Rachel, my… uh, companion."

Rachel moved to shake the girl's hand.

Naomi curtsied. "Welcome." Her gaze returned to Katherine.

Katherine gestured toward the nearby onlookers. "I'm pleased there aren't many people here. However, I find it unusual."

"Yes, My Lady. There was a commotion a few minutes ago, and most of them left for the upper deck." Naomi gestured toward the stairs at the center of the room. "I believe someone else has arrived."

"I hope it's not Father."

Naomi giggled softly.

Katherine glanced at her and frowned.

Naomi grimaced. "I apologize, My Lady. Uh, the dresses will be easy, but repairs to your ship or finding other air transportation will prove difficult. Almost all the men have been called to duty, and darts have been requisitioned for the fight. It might be easier to take the lift down and use the magrail."

Katherine pursed her lips. "No. You work on transport to Camden. Rachel and I will go to the shops to purchase clothes."

"Yes, Lady Katherine." Naomi curtsied and hurried away.

As they walked, Rachel leaned to Katherine. "Is Naomi your servant?"

"Yes, a helot, but she's been with our family since her birth. She's my ladies maid."

"Why didn't she want to go to this Camden place?"

Katherine smiled. "Camden is the family summer home in the mountains. This time of year it's usually empty. Right now I'm sure Naomi is on her ethercomm telling a dozen or more servants to hurry there and prepare the house."

She gestured toward the stairs, and together they proceeded down.

The floor below reminded Rachel of the stores in an airport. Several restaurants and pubs lined either side along with gift shops and other establishments that catered to last-minute or forgotten items. Rachel hadn't noticed any coins, paper, or cards that looked like currency. "What do you use for money?"

"Well, as the daughter of a marquis I could just have them bill Father, but," she held up her arm, "remember the bracelet?"

"Huh? The band works as money?"

Katherine looked about. "Use Lingua Terra as often as you can, or speak softly."

Rachel noticed the dozens of people watching as they walked along the corridor. She nodded.

Proceeding down the passageway, Katherine grinned. "To answer your question, the bracelet works as both cash and credit. Where you're from, do they have credit?"

Rachel noticed that Katherine avoided using the word Earth. "Oh, yes." She grinned. "Credit is a concept I'm familiar with."

After passing a few more shops, Katherine stopped in front of one. "I hate to do this."

"Do what?" Rachel looked first at Katherine and then at the store window filled with dresses that seemed right out of the Victorian era. Long gowns filled the window, most covered in lace and embroidery. The dresses looked heavy, hot, and confining. The sign above the door read, "Travel Clothing & Necessities."

"I hate to buy from this shop. Their frocks are rather ordinary, but the minute I buy from here they'll use it on all the vids as an advertisement." Katherine sighed. "Oh, well. I suppose it must be done."

They hardly passed through the door when three shop assistants surrounded them. All wore long, elaborate gowns similar to those Rachel had already seen. They curtsied as if they recognized Katherine. The youngest girl, about their age, giggled.

"I need two complete outfits." Katherine maintained a cool aloofness. "One for me and the other for my companion."

The three hurried off but returned in moments with gowns fit for a period movie.

Rachel moved around the store examining items and allowing Katherine to do the talking. Most of the shop displayed dresses, corsets, and women's shoes. The rest consisted of hats, combs, brushes, toiletries, luggage, and a few strange items she didn't recognize. The feel of the gowns varied; some felt like silk, others like taffeta.

"Show me that gown." Katherine pointed to a red dress nearby with elaborate swirls and folds.

Rachel moved closer and used the rudimentary Lingua Terra she had learned over the last couple of days, to listen and try to understand.

Pointing to another dress, Katherine said, "Let me see it." She stood before a nearby mirror.

The oldest woman tapped on a nearby screen.

The reflection in the mirror fluttered and then the dress appeared on the mirror image of Katherine. As she moved her arms, legs and body, the dress appeared to move with her. "This one may do."

While it amused Rachel to watch the various dresses appear in the mirror, she wished Katherine would pick one. She lost count of the number of virtual outfits her friend tried on. This sort of clothes shopping had always bored Rachel, and she had a multitude of questions that needed answers. Among them, was Lucas okay? How could they find out? Could they talk with him?

"Oh, that one will do." Katherine pointed to a gown she'd tried on twenty minutes earlier. "Now find a dress for my companion."

Rachel would've been satisfied with any of them. They just needed to blend in so they could travel to Camden.

Katherine walked toward a changing room with one of the assistants. "The style should show we're friends but not be overstated or outlandish."

Rachel wanted to object. She only needed something plain and simple so they could get moving but she wasn't sure how to say that in Lingua Terra and didn't want to use English. So, she smiled.

Nearly a half-hour later Katherine walked from the shop in an ankle-length blue dress trimmed with elaborate white lace. Rachel followed in a similar aqua dress. Despite the bulk and length, it weighed surprisingly little. However, the corset proved as tight and confining as she'd expected, although it seemed to bend and flex with her waist.

As they stepped into the passageway Rachel glanced over her shoulder, "Why do they have a store like that all the way up here in space?"

"Where you are from, do they never lose your luggage?"

"Oh, yes." Rachel grinned. "Some things are universal." She tugged at the corset and then stopped to look at her reflection in a window. "I feel more conspicuous in this Victorian gown then I did in the pilot uniform."

"Victorian?" Katherine cast a questioning look. "What do you mean?"

"Oh. On earth, in the time of Queen Victoria, long ago, women wore dresses like these."

Katherine looked at her own dress. "This is relatively modern. Not like the gowns my mother wore at our age." With a nod of the head she motioned for Rachel to follow. "And we do blend in now."

Rachel followed. "You wear things like this every day?"

"I'll never wear this rag again."

"Rag? Except for the corset, I think this is a lovely dress."

"It's a rather simple, common garment." Katherine smiled. "I might give it to Naomi."

Rachel tugged on her dress.

"Are corsets uncommon where you come from?"

"Very." Rachel tried to take a deep breath. "I've never worn one."

"What an interesting culture."

"Yes. I hope you get a chance to see it someday."

Murmurs and voices rose in the lane of shops.

Rachel turned to see a crowd approaching. Frightened at the sight of so many people she backed to the side.

Katherine didn't move.

Naomi ran ahead of the approaching crowd. About ten feet away she abruptly stopped and curtsied. "I've arranged the most excellent transport for you madam." She then backed to one side.

There, front and center in the approaching throng, strode a smiling Prince Draven.

Chapter 20

Onboard the Devon Sky Lift
Over Devon Prime

Rachel backed up against a shop window as Prince Draven led a throng of uniformed guards and civilians toward them. The sentinels formed a semi-circle as ladies, young boys, and older men crowded nearby.

Naomi drew near as Rachel continued her efforts to become one with the shop window.

Katherine curtsied, and Naomi quickly followed.

Rachel did her best, if somewhat wobbly, curtsey.

"I'm delighted to see you again, Lady Katherine." Prince Draven drew near and touched her arm. "I so enjoyed our dance together on Novam Terram."

"I did also, Your Highness." Katherine smiled.

"I hear that you are in need of transport home."

"It's nothing you, sir, should be concerned with. We can take the lift down and—"

"And use public transport?" He shook his head in disgust. "I won't hear of it. Follow me. I have a shuttle waiting that can take you home."

Prince Draven clutched Katherine's hand and marched away.

With her arm stretched out, Katherine hurried to catch up to him. "It really is unnecessary, sir."

Naomi rushed to follow.

The guard closest to Rachel gestured that she should move with them.

Prince Draven glanced over his shoulder as they caught up. "My shuttle is just ahead." With Katherine still in tow, Draven turned down a narrow passageway.

Naomi, three paces behind, matched the stride of Prince Draven and Lady Katherine.

The guards ushered Rachel down the same hall. She glanced back. Two guards followed right behind her; the others blocked the entrance to the passageway.

Prince Draven squinted at Rachel over his shoulder. "I've met you before."

"No," Rachel used a word common to both English and Lingua Terra.

Prince Draven smiled and slowed his pace as they entered the launch bay. Nearing a dart he stopped and turned to Rachel. "Since I first met you, I've known you were different. Then I received information that confirmed it. You speak English don't you?"

Rachel froze.

Katherine shook her head. "No, Your Highness, she doesn't. Where would a commoner learn such a thing?"

Prince Draven frowned at Katherine. "I'm nearly certain you know the language also." He motioned for the ladies to continue their walk. As they did, he returned his gaze to Rachel. "However, for you it is not the dead tongue of a destroyed world."

Rachel's stomach twisted into a knot.

He smiled at her. "A few days ago we fought side-by-side against the Valac."

"Yes." Rachel frowned, remembering how terrified he'd been and how little he fought.

"You saved my life."

In broken Lingua Terra she declared, "I've not told... anyone... about what... happened."

He sighed. "That makes what I must do a bit difficult." He stopped and fixed his eyes on her. "Information from Star Chamber sources reached me yesterday that a girl from Earth had escaped an Aux research facility. You are that Earth girl."

Rachel gaped at his statement. "Uh... yes... I am from Earth. I believe it still exists."

"Yes. I know it does."

Katherine and Naomi both gasped.

Prince Draven waved his arm and two guards advanced with lances pointed at Rachel.

Rachel extended her arms in a stop motion. In English, she announced, "If Earth still exists then the Mage have lied. When I was taken, billions of people lived on Earth."

Naomi fell to her knees. Tears streamed down her face.

Prince Draven shook his head. "I've known the truth about Earth for some time, but the Kingdoms of Terra would fall if that knowledge became widespread. Truth can set one free, but it can also get you killed."

"These ladies are traitors. Beat them all to death, and then secure the bodies in the dart and launch it. When the wreck is found, it must appear as if they all died in the crash. Do you understand?"

*   *   *

Seekers of Earth is a 38,000-word introductory novella to the Guardian Knights of Terra series. For more information about the series go to my website, www.KylePratt.me.

While you're there, sign up for my free author newsletter, and you'll be the first to know about my new books, discounts, and giveaways.

Thanks,
Kyle

Guardian Knights Lexicon

Aculeus stinger = The main personal weapon of the Valac. Unlike a scorpion, the stinger can be shot and quickly replaced by a new stinger.

Amplux = Laser.

Automatos = Automatic system. From the Greek meaning, "acting of itself." Any automatic system is said to be an automatos.

Auxilum = Centipede-like sentient beings that have a centipede like body. They are allies of the Mage. Auxilum is commonly shortened to "Aux."

Bioculus = Binoculars.

Computare = Computer.

Dart = A fast Terran planet-to-orbit shuttle. Depending upon the class, these are shuttle or deep space craft.

Curtana-class: high-value, long-range freighter.

Espada-class: short-range surface-to-orbit personal transport.

Rapier-class: armed military short-range fighter.

Sabina-class: luxury mid-range personal transport

Sabre-class: armed military mid-range transport

Ethercomm = Transceiver (a radio) commonly shortened to "comm."

Geller = A light-year. Named after the Terran scientist that calculated it using Aux astronomical equipment.

Holoview = Holographic projector.

Helots = A subjugated population of humans (see "Seekers").

Lance = Gun/Rifle. A military lance has three modes of operation. In setting one, depending upon the model, it shoots bullets or shells (like a shotgun). In setting two, the lance fires a wireless electro-shock projectile something like a Taser. The third mode is an amplux (laser) beam.

Lingua Terra = The universal language of the Terran Kingdoms.

Magrail	= Magnetic Rail, similar to the magnetic levitation rail system.
Mage	= The overlords who provide the technology and coordinate the war against the Valac. Many commoners worship the Mage.
Mage Tunnel	= A wormhole.
Magshield	= Force field.
Medicus	= A military medic.
Monocular	= An optical instrument for viewing distant objects with one eye.
Palmcomp	= A handheld computer.
Seekers	= The Seekers of Earth, called helots by most people (see "Helot").
Skylift	= A space elevator.
Valac	= Scorpion-like sentient beings at war with the Mage, Auxilum and Terrans.
Vids	= Pictures or movies.
VidSet	= Television or video screen.
Vox	= A voice announcement system.
Wasp	= A Valac frighter craft.
Web	= A network of Computares or ethercomms.

Also by the Author

Recall the Earth (The Guardian Knights of Terra, Book 2) The Mage and the elite of Terra decree that the secret of Earth's existence must never be revealed. Prince Draven is willing to kill anyone who knows more than they should, but when Rachel and Katherine believe death is imminent, unexpected allies appear. Rachel dares to hope that she might see Earth, and her family, again.

* * *

Titan Encounter Justin Garrett starts one morning as a respected businessman and ends the day a fugitive wanted by every power in the known universe. Fleeing with his 'sister' Mara and Naomi, a mysterious woman from Earth Empire, their only hope of refuge is with the Titans, genetically enhanced soldiers who rebelled, and murdered millions in the Titanomachy War. Hunted, even as they hunt for the Titans, the three companions slowly uncover the truth that will change the future and rewrite history.

About the Author

Hello, and thank you for reading.

I grew up in the mountains of Colorado and went to Mesa State College in Grand Junction. When money for college ran low, I enlisted in the United States Navy. I thought I would do four years and then use my veteran's benefits to go back to college. Life often doesn't go as we plan it.

While serving in the navy, I wrote space opera and military science fiction stories. Both *Titan Encounter* and the *Final Duty* stories fall into that period.

My first assignment was with a U.S. Navy unit at the Royal Air Force base in Edzell, Scotland. Two years later, while on leave in Israel, I met Lorraine from Plymouth, Devon, England. We married the next year. Together we spent the remainder of my twenty-year naval career traveling across the United States from Virginia to Hawaii and on to Guam, Japan, and beyond.

After I retired from the military, I taught in an Alaskan Eskimo village for several years while continuing to write.

My first post-apocalyptic novel, *Through Many Fires*, became an instant hit, rocketing onto the Kindle Science Fiction Post-Apocalyptic list and eventually making it to the number one spot. The second book in the series, **A Time to Endure**, appeared on several genre bestseller lists and led to the recently released third book in the series, **Braving the Storms**. My books are available on all major online retailers

Today, Lorraine and I live on a small farm in Western Washington State. You can learn more about me on my website, www.kylepratt.me.

If you like what you've read

I am an independent writer, so I don't have an advertising budget. If you've read one of my books and found it entertaining, please tell your friends. Also, the more favorable reviews a book has, the better it sells. So if you liked the story, please consider writing a review on the site where you downloaded this ebook. If you don't like the story, please tell me why.

About the Newsletter

Once a month I send out an email newsletter about upcoming books, events, specials, giveaways, promotions, and more—and I give a free ebook just for signing up! Use the link below. I respect your privacy and will never rent, sell, or give away your personal information.

Newsletter: www.kylepratt.me/contact/